The bed was soft with quilts, and Peg fell into them still encased in the blue bathrobe. She watched Lauren unselfconsciously strip off her clothes. Peg's first impression was of size — the substantial breasts, the breadth of shoulders and hips covered with solid flesh.

Neither spoke, as if fearing that would break the spell. Lauren pulled the quilts back, rolling Peg under them. Then held her so close that Peg had trouble breathing, only letting her go long enough to open the bathrobe. When their skin touched in naked embrace, Peg felt absorbed by the warm, smooth fullness.

This was nothing she wanted to hurry up, she realized as they explored each other. When Lauren rolled her onto her back and gently ran a large hand from her breasts to her belly to the joining of her legs, Peg felt herself figuratively pinned in place. A puppet. The sound of their breathing filled her ears. Shivering under the touch, she moved in rhythm to Lauren's fingers.

D1502050

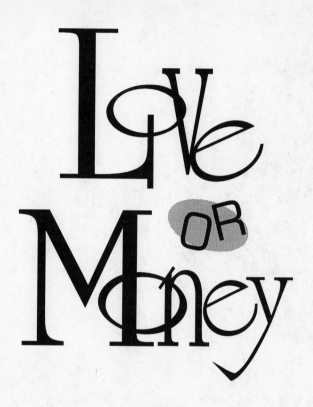

LOVE OR MONEY

BY
JACKIE CALHOUN

LOVE OR MONEY

BY
JACKIE CALHOUN

THE NAIAD PRESS, INC.
1996

Printed in the United States of America on acid-free paper
First Edition

Editor: Lisa Epson
Cover designer: Bonnie Liss (Phoenix Graphics)
Typesetter: Sandi Stancil

Library of Congress Cataloging-in-Publication Data

Calhoun, Jackie.
  Love or money / by Jackie Calhoun.
      p.   cm.
  ISBN 1-56280-147-3
  I. Title.
PS3553.A3985L68   1996
813'.54—dc20
                                                          96-26686
                                                               CIP

For Diane

About the Author

Jackie Calhoun is the author of *Lifestyles, Second Chance, Sticks and Stones, Friends and Lovers, Triple Exposure,* and *Changes.* She has stories in the anthologies *The Erotic Naiad, The Romantic Naiad, The First Time Ever,* and *Dancing in the Dark.* She lives in Wisconsin with her partner.

Although some of the locations in this book are actual places, the characters and story are fiction.

I
April 26, 1994

Peg was fucking Lauren.

Sylvia found it incredible that this was happening to her again. *She,* who was Sylvia Everett — successful, attractive, smart. Lauren barely had two dollars to rub together and even less in the looks department. Livid with anger, Sylvia faced the corner of the living room, her arms crossed, eyeing black dots in the sandstone paint. Silence consumed her as she remembered all Peg's past wrongs. Peg had left

Sylvia without a word. It had been days before she realized she wasn't coming back.

"I'm sorry. I can't explain it," Peg said, her voice small.

Sylvia caught a glimpse of Peg's white face, and anger, opening wide the valves in Sylvia's heart, sent blood thumping through veins and arteries. If she had a stroke, it would be Peg's fault. With shaking fingers she pressed the ache in her temples. Didn't it matter that they owned this house, that they'd been together seven years? She banged open hands against the wall. More dots appeared in the paint. "Why?" she demanded.

Peg showed her a helpless shrug. "I love her."

Sylvia stared disbelievingly at Peg, who was leaning against the door frame hugging herself. Peg's dark blue eyes looked almost black; her short brown hair stood on end. It was a habit of hers, to run her fingers through its thickness.

"You don't love *me*?" she asked.

Peg whispered, "Yes, I love you."

"That big, sloppy cunt. She thinks she's got talent. Those gaudy paintings of hers don't even look like anything." Having spat out the words, she wiped her mouth with the back of her hand. She wished she'd never praised Lauren's stupid work. At least, she hadn't meant it.

"Why do you always put people down?"

Restless anger pulsed through her system. Sylvia attempted to check the ebb and flow of it, to gain some control. "She's the worst kind of sneak. If she ever lays another finger on you, I'll cut it off."

"I'm just as much to blame."

"Yeah, you are. You're too stupid to know what's

2

good for you." Curling her fingers, Sylvia hit herself on the chest with such force she winced. "Who earns most of the money here? I run my own business. What do you do? You read other people's work." She made it sound like the most menial of jobs. It was, compared to her own. She'd made her mark here in the Fox Cities, and in Wisconsin. "If we had to live on your salary, we'd starve."

"Just calm down, will you?"

She clutched herself to stop the shaking and yelled, "How calm would you be if I had an affair? You'd better not have done it in our bed." She moved closer, threatening.

Peg turned and walked toward the door. "I'll come back when you've gained some control."

"Where are you going? To see her?" Gripping Peg's arm, she heard herself pleading. "Don't leave. Please."

"Let go." Peg shook free. The door banged behind her.

Sylvia followed, shouting as Peg's blue Ford Tempo whipped out of the driveway and sped down the street, trailing exhaust. "Go ahead and fuck her. You're both sluts."

Breathlessly, she slammed back inside and burst into tears. She never cried alone for long, though. After a few moments, she called work. She'd left before four. Her secretary should still be there.

"Judy, clear my schedule for tomorrow." She listened impatiently. "I don't care if the President of the United States wants to see me. I won't be in."

The clawing inside drove her back to the phone. She always called someone when she and Peg had a disagreement. Talking it out with one of her friends

3

calmed her. Her voice broke when Deirdre answered. "Peg's having an affair."

A brief silence followed. "Are you sure?"

Did Deirdre think she would lie? Sarcasm tinged her voice. "I caught her necking with Lauren Platt in my living room. I threw that sneaky cunt out." Resolutely, she banished the mental picture of their embrace. She had known Peg had been given the day off, it being her thirty-seventh birthday. She had planned to surprise her, not be astounded herself.

Deirdre apparently misunderstood. "Maybe they were just hugging."

She gave a harsh laugh. "Peg admitted they were doing it."

"Did you tell Peg to pack her bags?"

"I just want everything to be the way it was." Her throat filled. "Tell me the truth. Do I deserve this? Aren't I still pretty good looking?" She knew she was. Even at forty-eight, she had hardly any wrinkles. And her hairdresser managed to match the natural auburn her hair once had been. Peg already had more gray than Sylvia had shown at her age.

"Do you want me to come over?"

A car door slammed. She glanced out the window, saw the Tempo once again in the driveway. "Got to go. Peg's back."

The kitchen door opened, letting in the cool damp carried by the river. "I came to get some things. I won't be back tonight. We'll talk tomorrow after work." Peg started for the stairs.

"You won't be working if you walk out on me. I'll destroy you." A controlled rage gripped Sylvia. Except for the slight quiver in her voice and her shaking

4

hands, she might have been telling Peg what was in the mail. Her calm made her proud.

Peg turned, one hand on the bannister. "How?"

"I'll tell your boss, your parents, your brother, Lauren's boss, her parents." Her facial muscles began to twitch, and she clamped a hand over her cheeks.

"Tell them what?" Peg asked quietly.

"That you're lesbians." She changed tack. "Don't leave me alone tonight. Please."

"You'd be admitting that you're a lesbian too."

"I don't care." Why should she care? No one could fire her. And cheaters deserved to be exposed.

"You threaten to out me, yet you ask me to stay," Peg said angrily. "No way."

"I want to die." It came out as a wail, surprising even Sylvia.

"All right, all right. I won't go tonight."

Relief left her weak. It always worked. But then she remembered why she'd said it, and she wanted to tear Peg's head off as much as she longed to hear her beg forgiveness. Watching her climb the stairs, she followed. She would clean the bathrooms, just in case Lauren had used them. And change the sheets. And paint over those black dots on the living room wall.

Peg felt trapped, rooted by guilt. She should have kept driving instead of coming back to get her things. Now she wouldn't be able to leave tonight. She'd thought Sylvia would show her the door, not beg her to stay. It had been a terrible shock for all three of

5

them, and Peg desperately needed to talk to Lauren. Remembering the distress on Lauren's face, she ached to know if she was all right. Had she herself looked so alarmed?

Then, unwillingly, she recalled the changing expressions crossing Sylvia's face before the mask of anger slipped over it. The rarely glimpsed vulnerability revealing the warmth of an expected welcome, quickly replaced by astonishment, followed by pain, and ending with rage. She'd seen for a moment the woman she once had loved, the woman for whom she still felt the loyalty of a shared past, and knew the extent of her betrayal.

Looking up, she glimpsed blue through the skylight. She loved the house. It would be hard to leave it. Sensing Sylvia close behind her, she turned. "Why are you on my heels?"

"We need to talk." Sylvia's eyes snapped blackly in a face of angles and shadows, her mouth a thin, pink line. Her hair looked a little too red this time. The sun did that, some chemical reaction with the dye.

"All right. Over supper. Okay?" She glanced at her watch, surprised to see it was not yet six. "I'll fix something. I just want to change clothes."

"I'm not hungry," Sylvia said peevishly.

Peg dragged herself up the oak staircase. "Neither am I, but we have to eat." God, how she wished it were tomorrow. Going to work had never been so appealing.

"I'm going to clean everything she ever touched." Sylvia's penchant for cleanliness bordered on obsessive.

The words brought with them a memory of

Lauren's sweet touch and with it a brief smile. Could she give that up? She needed to think about where they would go from here, because there was no turning back. "Why?"

Sylvia was standing in the bedroom door, shaking again. "Where did you do it? How many times?"

Sighing, Peg turned away and unbuttoned her blouse. As she did, she felt strong fingers gripping her shoulders.

"Don't you dare turn your back on me." Then Sylvia's voice dropped to a seductive whisper. "Let's make love. Now."

Heart pounding, Peg pulled away and quickly changed into jeans and sweatshirt. "I'm going to start dinner." She grabbed a pair of tennies and clambered downstairs. Hearing Sylvia follow, she muttered, "Fuck." There was no escaping.

In the kitchen she pulled the marinating chicken breasts out of the fridge. She'd had a promising meal planned. Damn, she thought. Damn, damn, damn.

"Want some help?" Sylvia hovered nearby.

"I thought you were going to clean." Peg desperately needed a few moments alone to collect her thoughts.

"I can do that later."

"Do it now." She rummaged for salad makings and looked in the cupboard for pasta.

"Don't tell me what to do."

Peg winced. "Okay. Do whatever you want." Keenly aware of Sylvia's presence, she busied herself with the chicken, started water to heat for the pasta, cut up vegetables for salad.

"Was she good?"

"What?" The knife slipped and nicked her thumb.

"I'll get a bandage."

"No. I'll just wrap it in paper towels. It's nothing."

"Was she a good lover?" Sylvia looked like a Picasso painting with eyes and mouth awry, arms and legs and breasts oddly placed.

Sighing, Peg tried to avoid answering. "Why would you want to know that?"

Sylvia stepped closer. "As good as I am?"

She paused, weighing her answer, and found she couldn't deny Lauren. "You don't want to know." A whisper.

Spinning away, Sylvia ran from the room. A high, thin wail stayed behind.

* * * * *

1991

Smiling grimly as Peg gripped the door handle and pushed imaginary brakes, Sylvia zipped through traffic on Highway 41. She cut in front of a truck in order to pass the car in front of her, then pulled back into the right-hand lane. Horns blew.

"Slow down, will you?" Peg said through clenched teeth. "You're going to kill us both and maybe someone else."

"Good. I want to die," she said. "I went to your goddamn banquet just to please you, and then all you do is criticize me." Peg had dared tell her to lighten up, that she was embarrassing her.

"Well, I'm not ready to die. Take it easy." Peg

glanced at her. "Why did you jump all over Robb? He was just kidding."

Sylvia held the steering wheel in a death grip. Driving like this scared her too. "He said stupid things about women spending money frivolously. He owns a snowmobile. What could be more extravagant? His wife works. Why shouldn't she have nice clothes?"

Peg sighed. "All right, all right. I apologize. Now slow down."

"You said *I* embarrassed you. I at least stand up for what I believe in. You should be on my side. I always defend you, even when I don't agree with you." Right or wrong she invariably stood with Peg.

"It wasn't a matter of taking sides or standing up for something. You always take everything everyone says so seriously."

"First I embarrass you, now I take things too seriously. Do I do anything right?" God, the gall of it.

Peg said, "Why don't you let me drive?"

"Fine. Good. I suppose you do that better too." She pulled onto the berm, setting off a chain reaction of horns blowing and brakes screeching. Throwing the shift lever into park, she jumped out. She made her way through a ditch and up a short hill.

As Sylvia scaled a fence, a police car, its blue and red lights flashing in the night, pulled up behind her Volvo. She walked away, leaving Peg to face the music.

* * * * *

9

"What's going on, lady?"

Peg shook her head and shrugged. She wasn't going to cover for Sylvia's crazy behavior. "She ran off."

"You weren't driving?" His voice reeked of suspicion.

"No. I don't drive like that."

When Peg unlocked the door to the house, the phone was ringing. She had been chastising herself, as she had many times, for not buying a home by herself. Why hadn't she listened to her friend Lisa, or paid attention to her own instincts? Why had she instead purchased this place with Sylvia? Too bad Lisa had moved away. She could use some advice right now.

"Come get me. I'm at the Red Bull." Sylvia sounded furious. "Why did you drive off without me?"

"Take a taxi. I'm not rescuing you this time." There'd be hell to pay, but something had to change.

"I'll just have another drink then. Maybe someone here will drive me home. Fuck you." Sylvia slammed the phone down.

"Fuck you too," Peg said to the cradled receiver.

When they went to the art show on Sunday, they were in the throes of an uneasy truce. Sylvia was punishing Peg in her usual way, with insults and silence. That was the pattern, until Peg couldn't stand the isolation anymore and did the making up herself.

Once inside the gallery, the blue funk Peg had sunk into Friday night after the banquet vanished. She stood struck by the vibrant colors. Pulsing with life, the warm images jumped out of the frames. She poured herself a cup of coffee and sat on a padded bench in the center of the room, where she could absorb the art with only a change of position.

She was aware of Sylvia circling the room, putting on the charm. When Sylvia led a tall woman wearing high-top tennis shoes to her, she knew she had to be the artist. No one else would dress in baggy cotton slacks and a T-shirt that read: *One Planet for All.*

"Lauren Platt, Peg Doyle." Then Sylvia turned to another woman and introduced herself, adding, "I own Everett Employment Agency."

Just like Sylvia to advertise herself at someone else's show, Peg thought, even as she said, "Wonderful paintings. Such brilliant colors. It's like they're alive."

"Thanks," Lauren said, and gave a throaty laugh, her eyes as bright a blue as if she'd painted them herself.

"I guess I sound like the novice I am." Peg wasn't a gusher by nature and had complimented Lauren sincerely. Somewhat miffed, she smiled uncertainly.

"I'm sorry. I always laugh when I'm nervous. It's great when someone walks in and shows genuine enthusiasm."

"Well, I've often wondered what it's like to have a talent. If it becomes a need you have to fulfill, whether you can ignore it."

"I can't. I've tried." Lauren shrugged, smiling wryly.

She studied her, wondering how the woman had the nerve to appear so indifferent to society's dictates. She and Sylvia had changed from sweats and tennis shoes to slacks and blouses and loafers. Lauren looked untidy from her high-tops up to her unruly, dishwater blonde curls and was apparently unbothered by it.

On the way home Sylvia said, "She needs someone to take care of her, doesn't she?"

"She doesn't have someone?" Peg negotiated through traffic. She had promised herself Friday night that she wouldn't willingly get into Sylvia's car again.

"I don't believe so." Sylvia darted a look at her. "What do you think about her paintings?"

"I loved the colors." Peg pictured Lauren in her too-large clothes, wondering if they were meant for comfort or concealment.

"She is talented."

"Where did you meet her?"

"Deirdre introduced us when we went out to lunch a couple weeks ago. Lauren was with some guy, Jimmy something-or-other." Sylvia shot her another glance. "She's one of us, you know."

"I thought so. I don't know why exactly."

Reaching across the seat, Sylvia took her hand. "Are you sorry?"

She resisted the urge to snatch her fingers back. "Sorry about what?"

"Friday night."

"Yes, I am." She was sorry for Sylvia's bad behavior, not her own reaction to it.

Sylvia cocked her head and offered her a long-toothed smile. "Let's make up then."

Peg had for some time viewed that grin as phony. Sighing, she squeezed and released Sylvia's hand. It was easier to swallow her own pride and disappointment than challenge the peace offering.

Sylvia had magnanimously decided not to hang on to her anger over Friday night, to let it go. Actually, she couldn't recall exactly what had been said. She couldn't even remember who had given her a ride home. She turned her head and looked out the window, pleased that Peg had been so reasonable, and thought that all she had to do was smile irresistibly.

"To be perfectly honest, I don't really like Lauren's paintings." She found them unsettling more than anything else. All those bright colors and abstract shapes. There was no order to them. One couldn't pick anything out and identify it.

The next day during her lunch hour Peg returned to the gallery on Morris Street. The paintings were still there, and she again sat on the bench in the middle of the room to let their colors wash over her.

After she'd spent the morning being extra nice to everyone who had been at the banquet Friday night, Robb told her not to worry, that no one held her responsible for Sylvia's behavior. Somehow, it made her feel worse.

"Here you are again. Fancy that."

So lost in thought, she jumped and frowned and took a moment to relocate herself to the present. She shouldn't have been surprised to see Lauren. After all, it was her exhibit. "My office is downtown. Thought I'd have another look-see. I like your work."

Lauren wore the same clothes she'd had on the day before. "Want to do lunch?"

"I brought my own." She lifted the bag with the sandwich and banana in it. "I didn't think I should eat in here."

"Let's go outdoors. It's too nice to be inside anyway."

Between the gallery and the neighboring building was a small green space with a slender mountain ash that was uncurling new leaves and a park bench dedicated to a former councilwoman. Lauren plunked down and patted the seat next to her. "You can eat here." She sniffed the air. "Thank god it's April. Finally, a little color here and there."

Peg looked down at grass sending fragile tendrils toward the sun. A soft breeze ran warm fingers through her hair, and she raised her face toward the light. She had walked right past the tiny park without giving it a second glance.

Lauren was looking at her, her eyes a blue squint in the cloudless day.

"Want to share my banana and sandwich?"

"That what you usually eat for lunch? I'd starve." Lauren grinned.

"It doesn't look like you're eating anything."

"When you go back to work, I'll run over to the university cafeteria. Where do you work anyway?"

"At Binery Inc. I'm a proofreader."

"Really? Something like an editor. God, I can hardly put a sentence together right. I'm impressed." Lauren's face lit up.

Her own laugh scoffed. "I read mostly textbooks and instruction manuals. Pretty boring stuff."

"You catch mistakes, make corrections. Right? I couldn't do that."

Peg smiled a little at her own pleased reaction, even though she knew Lauren's response to her relatively mundane job was overenthusiastic. "Well, I certainly couldn't support myself your way, by painting."

Lauren roared with laughter. "Neither can I. I teach art classes at the university. I make enough to get by." She was frowning now. "Remember when you asked me if I had a need to create? It's expensive to do what I do. Art supplies are costly." Shrugging, Lauren's face cleared.

Peg had been fishing for information, pretty sure that Lauren paid the rent and bought the groceries some way other than by selling her art. She looked reluctantly at her watch, saw it was time to leave.

Shifting on the bench, Lauren said, "Hey, can we do this tomorrow? I'll bring my own lunch."

"Why not?" She was surprised not only by her own pleasure at the suggestion but by her quick response.

"Let's meet here at noon."

"Sounds good."

II
April 27, 1994

Sylvia stared at her reflection. She looked like shit, but who wouldn't after crying all night? Jesus, she felt terrible. Her head throbbed; her arms and legs had become rubbery appendages. At least she didn't have to go to work, but what would she do all day if she stayed home? Peg had resembled death warmed over and still had gone to work. Well, if she herself couldn't sleep, why should Peg? It was her fault they were awake anyway.

She sat on the toilet and rubbed her head. No matter how many questions she'd asked, she hadn't been able to get any more information out of Peg. When Peg had occasionally slid into sleep, Sylvia had wakened her. She'd made Peg promise not to see Lauren today, telling her that she'd call the university if she did. She would too. She'd tell them Lauren was seducing the female students. It was okay to protect your home whatever way you could. The old cliché about any weapons being fair in love and war applied here.

Phoning the university, she asked for Lauren's office. Slut. What did Peg see in her anyway? She just couldn't imagine. The woman was a slob. She always looked a mess.

Lauren sounded breathless. "I've got about two minutes."

"Well, then listen well. I'm going to expose you any which way I can think of if you don't stay away from Peg."

A few relishing moments of heartbeating silence followed.

"Go ahead."

She was prepared for this. "Then I'll expose Peg."

Another lengthy pause ensued, while she toed black dots on the floor. She'd have to scrub them off. When she'd gone to paint the living room wall, she hadn't been able to find those spots she'd seen yesterday. It seemed like all she did was clean.

The phone clicked dead.

She immediately called Peg at work. "I just talked to Lauren. I told her if she doesn't leave you alone I'll expose her."

More silence. The power lay in not being afraid to

17

use any measures. That's why Sylvia was so successful in business too.

"I can't talk right now."

"We'll discuss it this evening."

"There's nothing to discuss. If you do that to Lauren, I'm gone."

Peg set the receiver down ajar. She knew Sylvia would most likely call back.

"You all right?" Robb asked, squeezing her shoulder on a return trip from the coffeemaker. "I hate to say this, but you don't look so hot. Maybe you should go home."

Home was the last place she wanted to go. "I'd rather die," she muttered.

"That bad, huh?"

"I can't talk about it." On top of being so tired, her nerves jittery from too much coffee, she was filled to the brim with despair. She certainly couldn't explain any of this to anyone else, and now she was cut off from Lauren.

The receptionist paged her to the lobby at noon. She went with her heart in her throat, fearing Sylvia might be waiting. Lauren stood staring out the front window. Her old GMC half-ton truck with the battered cap was parked across the street. They drove to River Park and sat on a bench watching the water rocket past.

Lauren asked if she'd heard from Sylvia that morning.

18

"Of course." She glanced at Lauren and wanted to run fingers through her wildly curling hair. Sylvia thought her unkempt; Peg saw her as endearingly unselfconscious. "I'm sorry."

Lauren took her hand and turned it over. "You're not responsible for what she does."

"You didn't sleep last night either, did you?" It showed in the faded blue of her eyes.

"How could I, what with worrying about you? What happened after I left? Maybe I should have stayed."

"It's good you left. She went on a tirade, of course, but it would have been much worse if you'd been there, and I'm used to her anger. She kept me up all night, though."

"The worst part is not being able to get in touch with you."

"I know." Her eyes settled on the rushing river, carrying its debris northward. Mallards and Canada geese bobbed on the current that fell over and folded back on itself, creating whitecaps and roiling eddies. "I should have told her long ago, but I didn't have the nerve. Now we both know why."

"When I saw her in the doorway, I thought my heart had stopped."

"Me too." With a pang, she once again pictured Sylvia as momentarily defenseless. "I just wish we'd denied it." She struggled against a terrible sense of doom.

"How could we do that?"

"By pretending it was just a friendly hug." It never paid to be honest with Sylvia.

"Now what?"

"She'll do just what she says she'll do. You might be better off if I don't see you again."

Lauren stared at her intently. "Is that what you want?"

She'd be doing her a favor to say yes. But she found she couldn't. "No. But you'd be safe from her wrath."

A small smile dimpled Lauren's cheeks. "Sacrifice yourself, would you? Don't do it for me. I don't like martyrs. Don't trust them either."

"I wish we could go to bed." There would be comfort, at least, in physical contact.

* * * * *

1991

Sylvia answered the phone. "Thanks. Sounds good. Let me ask Peg." She covered the receiver. "Lauren invited us to eat at her place Friday night. Do we have any other plans?"

"I don't think so. Check the calendar." Lauren had told her she was going to ask them to dinner. They'd been having lunch outside the gallery now for close to a month.

"What time do you want us there, and what can we bring?" Sylvia asked. "Six o'clock and nothing? I need directions, though."

Peg knew where Lauren lived. Although she hadn't been inside the place, she'd driven past.

Friday night began badly. Sylvia wanted to drive. After a short argument, Peg gave in because she didn't want to spoil the evening.

Sylvia handed Peg a scrap of paper with scribbling on it.

She studied Sylvia's writing. "This address is on the east side, near the campus."

"Just read the directions. Okay?" But then she snatched them from Peg. "Never mind. I'll read them myself."

They completed a huge circle and were already ten minutes late when Sylvia finally said, "Okay. You know so much, you get us there."

In a matter of minutes they were parked in front of an older, three-story house.

"You've been here before, haven't you?" Sylvia slammed the door of the Volvo, something she seldom did. She considered the car a sign of her success.

Peg thought of it as a tank that protected Sylvia from her own capricious driving. Sylvia never signaled, cutting off other cars without a second glance. "I've never been here," she said honestly.

A slender man with an overgrown flattop flung open the door. He grinned engagingly. "You are Peg and Sylvia, I presume?" When they nodded, out of breath from the climb to the top floor, he continued, "Yes, you're at the right place. I'm Jimmy, sent to answer the door by the cook who sensibly banished me from the kitchen. She said, however, if either one of you does salad, you're more than welcome."

Lauren had spoken to Peg about Jimmy, her longstanding friend. He'd gotten her through some bad times, she'd said without elaborating.

"Quite a climb, isn't it?" He resumed his monologue as they stepped inside. "Lauren says it's a compromise for exercise. I think it's downright inhospitable." Still grinning, he stood in the middle of a room that would have been stark were it not for the walls, which were covered with Lauren's art.

"Hi. Sorry about the stairs." Lauren appeared in the doorway to the kitchen. "This apartment was the best price in town. A real bargain."

"I make salad," Sylvia offered, glaring briefly at Peg.

Peg returned the look, knowing Sylvia would rather think she had lied about being here before than admit she was lousy at following directions. "If you want an extra hand, let me know."

"Jimmy will show you the place, won't you, sweetcakes."

Cute, Sylvia thought, following Lauren into the kitchen, thinking maybe she was a fag hag. Some women just liked hanging around gay men. Discreetly appraising Lauren, she thought her on the large side — not heavy, but big boned. Tall with strong arms and wide shoulders, equally broad hips and ass that the baggy T-shirt and shorts made bigger.

"The salad makings are on the butcher-block table there. I'm running a little late. Hot, isn't it?" Wiping her cheek with an upper arm, Lauren kneaded dough. Pizza, she had said over the phone. She hadn't said it would be homemade.

"You must have the oven on. It smells wonderful in here." Sylvia began shredding lettuce into a bowl on top of the huge cutting block. "How did you get this up here? It looks like it weighs a ton."

"It does. I had a lot of help. Bought it at an

auction in Wild Rose last year. I hate to think about moving it."

The table had four broad legs and a top that was at least eighteen inches thick; its surface was covered with deep cuts as if it had suffered the blows of a hatchet. It wasn't a piece Sylvia would want in her kitchen.

Peg moved slowly around the living room. The walls were painted white. The dark uneven floorboards, highlighted by a few faded throw rugs, creaked with each step. The paintings lent color to the room.

With hands clasped behind his back, Jimmy matched his steps to hers, apparently as intent on Lauren's creations as she was. Side by side, they made their way around the living/dining room past the oak table and chairs, the pine Hoosier cupboard, the two beat-up easy chairs, the old couch, the end tables and lamps, the two large bookcases.

When they had completed the rectangle, he opened a door. "Let me show you her work room." He switched on track lighting and she blinked against the sudden brilliance.

Art materials were stacked against the walls, piled on the tops of shelving and windowsills. A sheet of plastic was spread beneath a table where two paintings were in progress. On another worktable stood a two-foot-tall clay sculpture of a woman. The figure was generously proportioned. She wondered if it was a self-portrait.

"Does she ever use models?" she asked.

He gave her a wry smile. "I posed for her once, in the raw."

"Peg had better not." Sylvia's voice startled them both into turning.

"He was a rotten subject, too. Forever scratching, always cold." Lauren stood next to Sylvia, dwarfing her.

Peg had never thought of Sylvia as thin until then.

"It was winter. I had mountains of goose bumps."

Lauren grinned. "You're just a wuss. Dinner's ready."

* * * * *

1994

In fact, Peg had posed several times during the fall of 1991. Lying in bed next to Sylvia, she got through the nights remembering how it had been. Sometime Sylvia had to sleep, and even when she was awake, there had to be moments of silence when it was possible to drift and dream. Those were few and far between since her duplicity with Lauren had been discovered.

Sylvia seemed almost manic with endless energy. She had always been slim, but now she was losing weight. They sat across the table from each other evenings and fought while the food got cold and their appetites dwindled. Eventually, Sylvia would scrape her plate's contents down the food disposal and Peg would feel obliged, after a few furtive mouthfuls, to do the same.

Peg stopped preparing good meals, resenting how the food was wasted. It had been more than two weeks since she and Lauren had admitted to their affair. Since then they had managed two clandestine lunches together, but only when she was certain Sylvia was occupied with clients.

"We can get past this," Sylvia said, cuddling close in the double bed, her free hand ranging over Peg's skin — hot and too quick.

"I'm tired, Sylvia." The open windows let in the street sounds and the white noise of distant factories. They lived in an elite section of town, across from Nicolet Park that fronted the river.

Instead of moving away, Sylvia shifted closer. "Let's make love. Please."

"We did last night. I'm not in the mood." She turned her back. Where Lauren was soft, Sylvia was bony. With each day it became more difficult to imagine Lauren in Sylvia's place.

When Lauren had asked her if she was sexually active with Sylvia, she'd replied with the truth. "When she insists on having sex, I shut my eyes and make love to you."

Sylvia curled against her, and Peg became rigid. "You're making me hot."

Stiffening, Sylvia rolled away. The tips of the maple tree branches scratched at the screen. "We need to get that tree trimmed."

"I'll call someone," Peg said, hating all this tension between them. "Good night."

"Let's talk like we used to. Just for a little while."

If they got to talking, it would lead to an argument and another sleepless night. Many more nights without rest and Peg would be in trouble at work. It was all she could do to stay awake while reading some boring text as it was. "I'm sorry, Sylvia. But I need to sleep."

Sylvia lay on her back, studying the ceiling fan. Its blades created shadows using the streetlight that filtered through the screens. Thinking that she had to beg for every scrap of attention, her heartbeat jumped from a walk to a trot to a gallop. When she heard Peg sleeping, her breathing deep and even, she couldn't stand the stillness.

Jumping to her feet, she went downstairs, switching on lights along the way. She turned on the CD player, rotating the volume to high. Since she couldn't sleep, she'd exercise. Going into the den, she pulled on the TV knob. She found Peg's dumbbells under the weight bench.

Moving in time to the music, she swung the weights in and out without regard to furniture or walls. She had always been so careful about her belongings that it gave her a perverse pleasure, a sense of freedom, to knock books and magazines off end tables.

When Peg tapped her on the shoulder, they both jumped away.

"Don't sneak up on me," she yelled. Then, "What the hell are you doing?"

Peg had already turned down the CD player. Now she moved around Sylvia and switched off the television. "Since when did you start lifting weights?"

"Since I can't sleep."

"Well, neither can I with all this noise and every light in the house on. Do you want to wake up the neighborhood?"

"Why not? I'll ask them if they've seen you fucking a big, sloppy bitch when I'm away." She relished Peg's stunned look. Peg should know she never minced words.

"What good would that do?"

"It would make me feel better."

Peg found Jimmy waiting for her outside work the next day. May had arrived without her noticing. The trees were blooming in earnest. The maintenance man was cutting the grass. Three years ago, when she first knew Lauren, she had glimpsed spring as a glory.

"I've got to ask you something," he said, walking with her toward her car.

"What, Jimmy?" She didn't mean to sound short, but the cumulative effect of over two weeks with almost no sleep and little food was a bad temper.

"What's going on?"

She snorted. "Lauren hasn't told you?"

"Can we go somewhere and talk?"

There'd be hell to pay if she was home late. Unlocking her car, she said, "Sure. Where do you want to go?"

Parking down by the marina at High Cliff, they sat side by side on top of a picnic table and watched waves wash up on algae-covered rocks. There was something soothing in the constant lapping sound.

He spoke first. "Lauren told me that you got

caught by Sylvia. I warned her this would happen sooner or later. It always does. You get careless. I know." He gave her a confiding look.

So, sometime or other he had been found in a compromising position too. "And what happened to you?" she asked, temporarily interested in something other than her own misery.

"I left him."

"Meaning, I suppose, that I should leave Sylvia." She sighed, realizing that her sighs were as much a form of conversation as her words. A cool wind tugged at her hair. She had decided to let it grow and had scheduled a perm for next week. Sun peeped in and out between fast-moving clouds.

"Well, that's my question. Why don't you?"

"What was this guy like that you lived with?" She looked at him, even though turning her head meant her hair blew across her face. He still wore his in an overgrown flattop. His eyes looked like deep puddles of mud, and his shoulders were hunched under a thin jacket. "Did you own property together?"

"He was a nice guy, and no we didn't."

"Well, Sylvia's not a nice woman, not now anyway, and we own a house and have a couple of joint bank accounts." She remembered the mean, crude edge to Sylvia that had appeared last night. She knew it was there; somehow, though, it always shocked her. But it was more than that. She felt that she was knee-deep in quicksand and sinking. Getting to work and doing a half-assed job took all the energy she could muster these days.

"All the more reason to leave her. Take half the money and run." He gave her a crooked grin.

She laughed. "Where to?"

"Lauren would gladly take you in."

Inhaling the smell of the lake, of water and fish and weeds, she felt something stir inside. "Jimmy, Sylvia means what she says. She'll try to destroy Lauren if I do that, and then me."

"By telling everyone you're lesbians?" His eyes flickered with anger. "Lauren's family knows."

Hers didn't, though. She was ashamed to tell them how deeply involved she was with someone who would use this knowledge against her. "Much worse than that. She'll claim that Lauren's seducing her female students."

"She's the lowest of the low then."

She started to disagree with him, and couldn't. But who wanted to think that the woman she had thought of as her other half for seven years would rather destroy her than let her go? Her affair with Lauren had begun over two years ago. No wonder she had kept it under wraps.

"She wasn't always like this," she said unconvincingly. "And remember, I cheated on her, not the other way around."

"How did you get involved with her in the first place?" he asked quietly. "Off the record."

"I just sort of drifted into it."

She had never met a driving force like Sylvia. She hadn't know at the time that this woman, who seemed so self-assured, had just bounced off another relationship. She had allowed herself to be wined and dined, impressed because Sylvia tossed money around with what seemed like wanton disregard. She knew better now. Heaven help the person who tried to separate Sylvia from her money.

"I need to go, Jimmy." She slid off the table.

"Give Lauren my love. I'll call her tomorrow from work."

"What are you going to do?" he persisted.

But she couldn't see beyond getting through tonight. "I don't know."

III
April 26, 1989

The closing had taken place that afternoon on Peg's thirty-second birthday. They were celebrating in their newly purchased home. Peg looked around the kitchen and saw the counters, the empty spaces for refrigerator and stove, the built-in dishwasher, the walls of oak cabinets, the windowed nook where they had set up a card table and two folding chairs.

"To us, Peg." Sylvia gave her the bottle of Dom

31

Pérignon to uncork and clasped her hands together.
"Are you scared?"

Somehow she never thought of Sylvia as scared.
Intimidating at times, coy at others, loving
sometimes, but never frightened. She stood up to
turn the corkscrew better. "Of what?"

"We're really together now." Sylvia moved nearer.
She put a hand on Peg's shoulder and gave it a
loving squeeze.

"That should make us feel secure, not afraid."
Shouldn't it? She wondered briefly if she was scared.
A little wary maybe. She'd argued with herself and
her friend Lisa when she and Sylvia were looking for
a place. Lisa had told her flat out that she was crazy
to buy a house with Sylvia.

"Anyone who gets angry when you call her Syl is
someone to look out for," Lisa had warned.

Lisa didn't know the beginning of it, she thought.
Sylvia's penchant for belittling those who disagreed
with her, including Peg, made her walk on conversational tiptoes.

"But, Lisa, we've been together two years," she'd
said. "It's time to take the plunge or get out. And I
have to give her the benefit of the doubt, don't I?"

"Why? If you have any doubts, take them and
run."

The cork popped, and she poured the smoking
champagne into flute-shaped glasses. "This is a new
start for us."

"I'll cherish you forever," Sylvia said, lifting her
glass to Peg's. "I changed my will. You get
everything I own."

The statement startled Peg. "Just the house will
do."

Sylvia said, "You need to make a will."

"I'll do that," she promised. "My half of the house and its belongings will go to you." Why were they discussing this? She feared it would blow the celebration to bits. "Shall we eat?" They had picked up Chinese carryout.

"Sure. Then let's walk through the rooms again and decide what goes where."

They moved into their new house the first day of May. When the furniture was in place and their friends had been fed Caesar's pizza, Peg and Sylvia made their bed and climbed into it as night fell.

The fan turned slowly overhead, chasing its own shadows. Dim light pervaded the room, and they lay listening to the neighborhood sounds: the steady hum from a distant factory, a faraway train, the occasional car passing, a dog barking nearby.

"Lisa doesn't like Deirdre, does she?" Sylvia said. Funny, she had never known that.

"They're different, is all. Deirdre's so serious." Peg made a tentative move toward lovemaking, caressing Sylvia's arm and shoulder.

"Lisa's so silly all the time." She could be a real asshole.

"She likes a good time. There's nothing wrong with making moving fun."

Irritated because Peg sounded annoyed, she crossed her arms. "She'd make a funeral fun."

"Let's not argue," Peg said appeasingly, reaching for her. She turned away, digging an elbow into Peg's ribs. "You don't want to christen the house?"

"You mean fuck?" Call a spade a spade.

"I mean make love," Peg said without enthusiasm.

"Not tonight."

"Would you like a back rub?"

She rolled face down. "Sure."

Sitting astride her hips, Peg massaged her shoulders and arms. Sylvia felt the skin bunching and straightening under Peg's fingers, and her breathing quickened. Gently, Peg kneaded her rib cage, her lower back, her buttocks, working her way downward. When Peg finally slid a hand up the inside of her thigh, she opened to her.

Trembling, she knew how wet she was. Sometimes she lost control like this, and later she would hate the weakness, but now she couldn't help herself. Stiffening a little as Peg's fingers slid inside, she attempted to turn. She felt too vulnerable in this position.

Peg withdrew, and Sylvia rolled onto her back. Peg leaned over to taste her breasts.

"Oh God, oh God, oh God." Sylvia whipped her head back and forth on the pillow. "I love it when you fuck me."

Peg was always so quiet when they made love. She never voiced her pleasure. It was almost like a reprimand, Sylvia thought as Peg quickened the rhythm of her stroking to match Sylvia's response. Her body bucked on the bed.

"Faster, faster. I'm coming. Ahhh." She jerked to climax and, spent, fell back on the pillow.

Her jaw ached from gritting her teeth. It took so much concentration, she felt released mentally and physically when it was over. During the act, she struggled to think about nothing, concentrating instead on sensation and her response to it, which became validated by her own voice. She wouldn't tell Peg what she had to blot out. How hard it was to let go.

"Your turn, sweetheart," she said.

"Just enjoy the aftermath. Lie still," Peg murmured, wrapping Sylvia in a hug and holding her until the small shivering spasms passed.

Then Peg closed her eyes and let Sylvia try to rouse her to orgasm. She thought tonight she would surely be able to make it. Once, she had been able to come in a matter of minutes. Now it required a lot of fantasizing. Her fantasies were becoming more bizarre. Several people occupied them, each invading her in some fashion. She would never admit these imaginings to anyone, she thought, while in the middle of one in which she was on her knees being tantalized by a tongue while dildoes filled her.

She asked Sylvia afterwards, "Do you ever fantasize when we're making love?"

"Do you?"

"I asked first."

"I picture us."

* * * * *

1994

Greeted by the tick of the kitchen wall clock and the humming refrigerator, Peg thought the house blessedly quiet. The light over the stove illuminated a note: LISA CALLED.

She had been meaning to phone Lisa, but she didn't know how to begin what she had to say to

35

her. She'd had imaginary conversations with her old friend during which she admitted: You were right, Lisa. I should have taken my doubts and run. Then she could have met Lauren on her own. Their love affair would have been legitimate from the beginning. She jumped when the phone rang.

"Ha, caught you finally." Lisa sounded much the same.

She smiled. "Had you waited a few more minutes you could have saved yourself the cost of a call."

"What the hell is going on anyway?"

"What did Sylvia tell you?"

"She bad-mouthed you big time. Said you were carrying on with another woman, that you'd betrayed her trust."

"Well, she has a right to be angry." She took a deep breath. "I got involved with someone."

"About time. Tell me about her."

Her smile grew into a grin. Trust Lisa to cheer her up. "She's a local artist who teaches at the university."

"A talented lady. And I bet she makes you feel good about yourself."

A sigh escaped. "Yes."

"You want me to come home and help you move?"

"I'd love to see you." She toed the floor, noticing how shiny it was. The house always looked magazine-picture clean. "But I can't move."

"Sure you can. We'll just box up your stuff, load it in a truck, and take it away."

If it were only that easy. "I own half of this house."

"Refinance. It happens every day."

36

"Sylvia doesn't want me to go."

"So? Tell her you're leaving."

She shook her head and, sensing another presence, lowered her voice. "You don't understand, Lisa. She'll try to destroy Lauren and me." And she told of the threats.

Silence. Then, "Call her bluff."

"She says she'll kill herself if I leave."

An explosive burst of air followed. "That's control shit. You can't be responsible for what she does. I'm getting in my car and coming home next weekend. We'll talk then."

Tears blurred the floor. She lifted her head and blinked. How could she explain that she was sunk up to her knees in quicksand? "Okay. Where do you want to meet? Not here." Maybe Lisa could get her out of the muck.

When Peg hung up and turned to go upstairs and change, she nearly choked on her heart. Sylvia was standing in the doorway.

"You told Lisa." It was a statement. Sylvia must have heard the conversation.

"You told her first. Where's your car?"

"Down the street. I walked through the park." Sylvia grinned humorlessly.

"You're spying on me." Peg made a mental note not to make phone calls from home again.

"You're the cheat, not me. Let me take you out to dinner. It's Friday. Maybe we can see a movie too."

"No, thanks." If dinner out was like dinner at home, they'd be screeching at each other over someone else's table. Sylvia never cringed from creating a scene in public. Peg gave her as wide a

37

berth as possible and started up the stairs to change clothes.

"I'll make us a nice supper then."

"I'm not hungry," she called over her shoulder. Peg was losing weight too. Even Lauren was shedding pounds. But Sylvia had lost the most, becoming a wraith of her former self.

Throwing herself onto the bed in the spare room where she kept her clothing, Peg thought how once she'd looked forward to weekends. Now it took all her energy to get through them. If she couldn't manage lunch with Lauren on Monday, at least she'd be able to talk to her on the phone.

Lifting her head at the sight of Sylvia in the doorway, she knew she had been foolish to be so dismissive about dinner. But for the life of her, she couldn't make herself say the right things anymore. In a moment of illumination, she got up and took a suitcase out of the closet. Going to her dresser, she dumped the contents out of her top drawers into the bag.

"What are you doing?" Sylvia's voice rose in pitch. Removing the clothes, she tossed them onto the floor. "You're not going to her. I'll wreck the house. I'll put your stuff out by the curb for the trash Monday."

"Cut it out. Let go." She tugged at the bra Sylvia clenched. It was one of Lauren's favorites, lacy and low cut.

"Please don't leave. I don't want to live without you." Sylvia pulled out the large middle dresser drawer to shove Peg's underwear on top of the clothes and noticed a pile of white envelopes. "What are these?" She grabbed them. "You've been writing to her."

"That's my mail. Put it back." Outraged, she jumped Sylvia. It was the principle of the thing that infuriated her, the invasion of privacy. There was nothing from Lauren in that mail. She kept those few cards and notes in her desk at work. These were letters from her family and Lisa.

Sylvia held her off until she looked through the envelopes, then tossed them back in the drawer. "You're hurting me."

Astonished by the older woman's strength, Peg thought it had to come from sheer will power. Peg was the one who opened jars, who mowed the lawn and shoveled snow off the walk, who rode her bike in the summer and skied in the winter. Sylvia had never shown an interest in anything athletic other than an occasional walk.

Panting and ashamed of herself for being physically aggressive, for showing uncontrollable anger, Peg straightened her clothes and ran fingers through her newly permed hair. It felt thick and untame. "You have no right to go through my things."

Sylvia's upper lip curled. "You're a sneak."

She stared at her for a moment. "You don't own me, Sylvia." She shook her head for emphasis. "I have a right to walk out of here."

"And if you do, you'll lose everything."

* * * * *

39

Monday morning Peg called Lauren from work. "What an awful weekend."

A long pause filled the space between them. "For me too."

"What's wrong?" Peg felt herself imploding, her heart bouncing like a yo-yo. She banked too much on Lauren's sympathetic understanding.

Lauren answered in a subdued, almost sullen voice. "I guess I expected something I shouldn't have."

"And what was that?" She knew, though. They'd had this conversation.

"I thought you would leave."

"I told you what it's like."

"Tell me again, I need to hear it."

"I'm afraid she'll kill herself or destroy you and me." She heard herself as she knew Lauren would — making excuses, even though the fears and threats were real enough. She could almost see Lauren's shrug.

"So, you're going to let her call the shots?"

"We have to settle on the house. I have a lot of money tied up in it and our joint belongings," she said, feeling desperate. "Can't we talk about these things in person?"

"When? I seldom see you anymore. I need to know something, Peg."

"What?" She wanted to rest her head on the desk and cry.

"What were we all about? Was it just an affair?"

"No," she protested. But then why couldn't she make the necessary moves to leave? "Let's meet at noon."

At River Park Peg took the parking space next to Lauren's truck, hiding the Tempo on the other side of the larger GMC. Walking to the bench where Lauren waited, she noticed that the river had slowed its northerly rush.

"Nice day, huh?" She looked for some sign of welcome.

Lauren gave her a distracted smile. "Yes."

Stretching her legs, she felt the sun's heat through her cotton slacks. "Be patient with me, Lauren. I'm stuck. I can't explain it any better. I should pack my bags and move out, I know, but I just can't do it. I feel so guilty." She thought of her aborted attempt to leave Friday night. Sylvia had dissolved her will with tears and pleading.

Lauren's blue eyes bored into her. "I'd think it would be a relief to walk away from that relationship."

Peg felt anger, which fizzled as soon as she spoke. "There were good times."

"When are you going to get unstuck?"

"Are you mad?" The best defense was an offense. She'd learned that from Sylvia.

"Frustrated. She's playing with us. Why don't you tell her to fuck off? I'm going to next time she calls."

"Easy for you to say." Here they were fighting. Lauren had been her refuge.

"Is it?" The blue eyes blazed. "She's threatened to tell my boss that I'm seducing female students. Do you remember that?"

Peg chewed on her lower lip, forcing back tears. "Yes. I told you it would be better if you didn't see me again. Remember that?"

Lauren leaned forward as if deflated. And frowned. "I can deal with Sylvia better than I can handle not seeing you."

"Be patient with me, Lauren," she said again. "I'm trying. I just can't seem to make decisions anymore." Surprised by unexpected tears, she absently wiped them away.

"Don't, Peg. I'm sorry. I'll wait."

Lisa had agreed to meet Peg at the Fox River Mall Saturday at noon near the theaters. The place was a zoo of bodies, mostly teenagers. Peg scanned the crowd for her friend's face, sure she would immediately recognize her.

"Hey there, lady. Looking for someone delightful, gorgeous, smart? Here she is."

She turned and was met by a wide grin, a smacking kiss on the mouth, and a crushing hug. "No wonder you snuck up on me. You cut your hair and lost how many pounds? No fair."

"Twenty-six to be exact. I went from a size fourteen to a ten." Lisa held Peg at arm's length. "I hate to say it, but you don't look so hot, kiddo. You can lose too much weight, you know. You could pose in an anorexic ad."

"Thanks." But an answering grin crept across her face. "You look marvelous — your hair, your clothes, the whole effect. How's your other half? I forgot to ask when you called."

"We have our ups and downs." Linking arms, Lisa

propelled her away from the crowded area toward the outside doors. "Shall we go somewhere less crowded?"

"Let's. God, it's good to see you."

"I have a feeling you'd say that about any ally at this point. Where to? I'm starved."

"Let's get subs and go to a park."

"Talk, girl. Tell me the whole story," Lisa said when they took their sandwiches to the Tempo and drove out of town toward High Cliff.

Telling Lisa about the past few years shamed her. "I'm such a fucking coward."

"Well, you're with the wicked witch of the Midwest. You have good reason to be afraid."

She half hoped that Lauren would be at the state park. She looked forward to running into her wherever she went these days, but it never happened. It had to be planned. "You always did make Sylvia out to be worse than she was."

"Did I? You should have left her long ago. Hell, you never should have been with her in the first place."

"You know how bad that makes me feel, Lisa? I don't want to think that there's nothing good about Sylvia. I've been with her seven years." She drove the road to the top of the cliffs, turned right and parked at the small lot where the blacktop curved toward the campgrounds. "Let's walk."

The wind off the lake climbed the cliffs and tugged at their hair. From way above the tree line, she studied the distant water and the boats on its surface that resembled toys.

She continued her defense of Sylvia and her own

involvement. "She's not all bad. No one is." But she'd noticed Sylvia's sharp edge early on, had been surprised by her mercurial temperament. Sylvia either loved you or hated you; there was no in-between. "How long can you stay?"

"Overnight. I'd hoped to meet Lauren."

"I don't know how we'll manage that." Sylvia's best friend, Deirdre, lived near Lauren's apartment. It wasn't safe to go there anymore. She felt wetness on her face and realized that she was crying again. "I'm sorry."

"Go ahead and cry." Lisa heaved a sigh. "What a mess."

"You're telling me." And she laughed. "I can't seem to make any decisions. You know? Instead I cry. A lot of good that does."

"You're probably depressed. Who wouldn't be?"

IV
1994

"I don't have time to correct your mistakes. This isn't a school." Sylvia slapped the letter on her secretary's desk. She was used to Judy's flinches and her apologies. She paid her well. There was no excuse for sloppy work.

"Sorry. I'll redo it."

"You bet you will, and this time get it right." Sylvia went back in her office and slammed the door. She was tired of mediocrity.

"Deirdre Walters, please." She swiveled her chair toward the window. Deirdre was a personnel manager for a health facility; she would understand. "It sure is hard to get good help, isn't it?" she began. They had talked about this subject often and were always in agreement. Even she, whose job was to find work for clients, couldn't hire a decent secretary for herself.

"You're not telling me anything. How was your weekend?"

"Not good. Lisa Davenport came to see Peg on Saturday. Remember her? She helped us move."

"She's something of a nitbrain as I remember."

"Yep. She regards life as a kind of joke. I called you Sunday."

"I was shopping. Dayton's had a sale."

"Want to meet for dinner tonight?"

She and Deirdre went back ten years to a NOW meeting they'd both attended after Sylvia first moved here from Milwaukee. She thought of this that evening while drinking a glass of Merlot at The Olive Garden while waiting for her old friend.

"Sorry to be late," Deirdre panted, sitting across from her and pouring herself some wine. "I need this like I need a sauna. It's hot out there." She was short and built like a box. Her face was broad, her features large, her skin coarse and now sweaty.

"Don't drink it then." It wasn't every day that she splurged on a bottle of wine.

"I shouldn't. But I love Merlot. Thanks." Deirdre's hand engulfed the wine glass as she raised it in a toast before drinking. "Where's Peg tonight?"

46

"At home, I guess." She couldn't watch her all the time. She'd tried that. Frowning at her glass, she took another swallow.

Deirdre gave her an appraising look. "You need to put on some weight, Sylvia. You'll get sick."

"Who cares?" She shrugged. No one did, really. Her family was far away, what was left of it — two estranged brothers. She needed to corner her friends again and rally them to her side. The trouble was that most of them were Peg's friends as well. "It's mid-June already." Nearly two months had passed since she'd found out that Peg had betrayed her. "I don't know what happened to the time."

Deirdre toyed with her napkin. The waitress had just left with their orders. "Look. Why don't you separate for a while? Tell her to leave. Then you can decide what to do."

She shook her head. "No way. She's not going to see that woman, not if I can help it."

"But wouldn't that be better than fighting all the time?" Deirdre looked like a bulldog, her brow wrinkled between wide-set brown eyes.

Sylvia pushed her chair away from the table. "I thought you were my friend." Whose side was she on anyway?

"I am, Sylvia. I just thought you'd be better off without Peg. Sit down. We won't talk about it."

Sylvia pulled her chair back in place as the waitress set bread sticks and salad on the table. While watching Deirdre fill her plate and eat ravenously, she nibbled on lettuce. Her appetite had shriveled into a tiny ball about the size of her

47

stomach, she guessed. Peg's fault, of course. She wondered if Peg would feel sorry for her if she took sick. Probably not.

* * * * *

Tuesday, October 15, 1991

Lauren begged until Peg finally gave in. "Okay, I'll do it. Next week."

"Tonight, now," Lauren insisted. "When will we have this much time again?"

Sylvia was out of town at a conference. They had just finished eating and were still seated at the oak table. Had she known this would happen? Lauren had been asking her to model for weeks now. "Let's clean up the dishes first." She got up.

"I'll do the dishes in the morning. Leave them." Lauren was at her side, taking the plate and glass out of her hands. "Come on." She pulled Peg toward the workroom.

She allowed herself to be towed along, realizing as she must have all along that her posing in the nude for Lauren would open the door to intimacy. No matter how professional Lauren professed such an act to be, it wouldn't stay that way. Deep inside, she knew it. And she was embarrassed.

Lauren handed her a bathrobe and left the room while she removed her clothing. There was a full-length mirror set on the wall by the door, and she looked at her naked body. It was small and neat. Her skin was smooth, her muscles taut, her nipples standing at attention. She ran her fingers over them, attempting to flatten them, but the room was cool.

Her bare feet could attest to that. She wrapped herself in the blue robe, noticing it would go around her twice. What was she so worried about?

"Stand over there under the lights, where it's warmer," Lauren urged her. "Don't worry about the robe, just drop it on the floor." Lauren sat in a director-type chair with a sketch pad on her lap, pencil poised over it.

Straightening and tucking in her belly with a deep breath, Peg let the wrapper fall to her ankles. She didn't look at Lauren, only heard her sharp inhalation. Years later she would remember it during the long nights that separated them, while recalling the words that followed.

"You have a beautiful body."

She didn't respond. Her figure was okay, it wasn't beautiful. Flashing a look at Lauren, she puzzled over her smile. It looked sad. Then, because she was still embarrassed, she dropped her gaze.

Quickly realizing that posing was work, she remembered Jimmy saying how difficult he found it was to remain motionless. She desperately wanted to scratch, ached with the need to move her muscles, and was soon chilled to the bone.

Somewhat chagrined, she understood that Lauren was serious about her work. Asking her to model hadn't been a ploy to get her clothes off. There was no clock in the room, and Lauren only talked when she spoke to her. Otherwise, she seemed totally preoccupied. Time slowed to a crawl.

When she thought she couldn't stand still another minute, Lauren suddenly jumped to her feet and rushed over to cloak her in the robe. "That better? You're almost as blue as the cloth. I'm sorry."

This was the closest they'd ever been to each other. She picked up Lauren's scent — the faint odor of her skin mixed with fabric softener and fresh air on her clothing. Sinking into the robe, she kissed her lips. It seemed as natural as anything she'd ever done.

When Lauren raised her head, her blue eyes had turned nearly black. "You sure you meant that? You aren't just grateful that I came to my senses and covered you up?"

It took the contact to know how good it felt. Nodding, she smiled. She knew better than to try to speak.

"If I'd known, I wouldn't have wasted all that time putting you on paper."

The bed was soft with quilts, and Peg fell into them still encased in the blue bathrobe. She watched Lauren unselfconsciously strip off her clothes. Peg's first impression was of size — the substantial breasts, the breadth of shoulders and hips covered with solid flesh.

Neither spoke, as if fearing that would break the spell. Lauren pulled the quilts back, rolling Peg under them. Then held her so close that Peg had trouble breathing, only letting her go long enough to open the bathrobe. When their skin touched in naked embrace, Peg felt absorbed by the warm, smooth fullness.

This was nothing she wanted to hurry up, she realized as they explored each other. When Lauren rolled her onto her back and gently ran a large hand from her breasts to her belly to the joining of her legs, Peg felt herself figuratively pinned in place. A puppet. The sound of their breathing filled her ears.

Shivering under the touch, she moved in rhythm to Lauren's fingers.

* * * * *

1994

Aimlessly, Peg wandered from room to room. She'd admired the two-story brick house long before she and Sylvia had ever seen the inside of it. The living room stretched from front to back with huge bay windows looking out at the park on one end, the backyard on the other. A raised brick fireplace, dominating one wall of the living room, opened into the den so that a fire could be built in both rooms. A formal dining room joined the living room to the kitchen toward the rear. The main entrance opened to a tile-floored foyer, which also linked living room to kitchen and off which were a closet and a half bath under the upstairs stairway. A porch with a railing spanned the front of the house, while a greenhouse-type smaller porch led off the kitchen and dining room. A side door connected the garage to the kitchen. There were three bedrooms and two baths upstairs and a full basement. Skylights over the second-floor stairs and the upstairs bathrooms provided natural light.

Knowing that this would not be her house much longer, she felt transient in it. Searching for an emotional reaction to this, she came up with only a sad emptiness. It all seemed unreal — the house, its furnishings, even herself. She left then.

She drove to Jimmy's place with no certainty that he would be home or that she would be welcome.

Surprised that she was doing this because she didn't believe in dropping in at people's homes uninvited, she hoped that perhaps Lauren would be there. He lived on the north side of the city in a renovated farmhouse, its few acres encircled by newly-built houses.

Flinging open the screen, he drew her inside and closed the door after a quick look up and down the street. "She's not following you, honey, is she?"

"I don't think so. Why?" Had she threatened him too?

He gave an exaggerated sigh. "I got a call from her the other day. She told me she'd get me fired if I took your side."

"Can she do that?" she asked doubtfully.

"I don't know. She finds employees for Dorn Advertising, where I work."

As a graphic artist, she knew. He and Lauren had attended art school together. He put an arm around her when she turned to leave.

"Come back here. I *have* taken your side. I told her to fuck herself with her broom. I can always work for my dad at the Orange Factory — squeeze juice, sell bagels. But I haven't forgiven him for naming me James." His last name was Jamison.

"I thought you were a junior." She smiled a little.

"I am, but doesn't that just make it worse?" He steered her toward the kitchen. "Let me fix you a strong one, put hair on your nipples."

"I don't want to pluck any more than I already do." It felt good to laugh.

"There, see, old Jimmy will lift your spirits. I hate drinking alone. You could move in with me."

"I'll keep that in mind." She sat on a stool at the

food bar while he poured two vodka tonics. It wouldn't be so bad, living with Jimmy. The house was large and bright. He was funny and kind.

"So, what's the latest development?" He handed her an ice-cold, tall glass.

She drank deeply. "Give me a minute. Tastes good. Thanks, Jimmy." A warm breeze wafted through open windows. On the horizon she saw lightning flash and listened for answering thunder.

"Don't you love summer? When I first moved here and started tearing this old house apart, I was surrounded by open fields that the weather rolled over. When the crops bent in front of the wind, you knew a storm was coming."

She smiled at the visualization. "I'll bet the winter winds were fierce."

"They shook the house. Lauren lived with me then." He was standing on the other side of the counter, smiling at her. He must have known she hungered to hear about Lauren. "She moved here to help when my lover was dying, and then she got a job and stayed on." He stared over her shoulder toward the window behind her, his light brown eyes shimmering. The wind was picking up. He blinked twice. "For some reason I never got HIV. I suppose I still could."

"How long ago was that?" she asked, wondering what it must be like to live with the knowledge that you'd been exposed.

"Five years, I think, maybe a little longer." He shook himself and focused on her. "I heard your friend Lisa was in town over the weekend. You should have brought her over."

She hadn't thought to do that, nor had she taken

her to Lauren's. Lauren had met them at Dooley's Restaurant Saturday night. "I will next time. I sure can't take her home. Lisa and Sylvia are like cats and dogs. Natural enemies."

"When are you going to get out of there, honey?" he asked.

Hearing her own sigh, she considered an answer. Maybe he would understand her dilemma. But she didn't feel like going into it. "We actually talked about my leaving the other day."

Sylvia had screamed in her face. "I want you out."

"I can't leave until we decide how to settle," she'd said, resisting the urge to rush upstairs and pack her bags.

"You don't deserve anything. I bought this house in good faith with you, and you cheated on me."

"You'll have to refinance, or we'll have to sell the house."

"No," Sylvia had stated flatly. "You're not taking my money and you're not leaving me for her."

"And how did that go?" Jimmy asked.

She looked at him. "Not well."

"Want to stay the night?"

"I can't." She dreaded going home. "I don't have any clothes for tomorrow."

She and Sylvia turned into the driveway that night one behind the other. The Volvo and Tempo parked side by side, as unlike as their owners. Her car made her think of the poor sister.

Sylvia unlocked the side door with shaking hands. "Where were you?"

"I went for a drive when you weren't home. Where were you?"

"None of your business. I sure wasn't with my lover." Sylvia's voice trembled.

"Neither was I." Humidity thickened the warm night. Rain began to fall in the arc of a streetlight. She followed Sylvia inside and locked the door. She had decided to sleep in her spare bedroom from now on; she headed for the stairs.

Sylvia pounded on the closed door, then pushed it open. "Why aren't you in our bedroom?" The room was dark except for light gleaned indirectly through the open windows.

Lying rigid in the double bed, Peg's inner warning system kicked into gear at the sight of Sylvia's spare figure in the doorway. She turned on her side toward the windows. Rain slithered down the panes.

"You don't want to eat with me, you don't want to talk to me, you don't want to sleep with me. You drive me wild. My head is pounding."

"It might help if you stopped yelling."

Sylvia pounced on the bed like an awkward cat, landing on hands and knees next to Peg. They rolled over twice and ended up on the floor with Sylvia underneath and screaming. "You're hurting me."

Peg scrambled to her feet and reached to pull Sylvia to hers.

Hitting at the helping hand, Sylvia struggled to stand. She placed one hand on her lower back. Her face twitched. "You're going to be the death of me yet." With a shove she sent Peg sprawling onto the bed. "Stay here then." She tucked her shaking hands under her armpits as she ran out of the room. A high-pitched wail tore from her throat.

Closing the door, Peg propped a chair under the doorknob. She slid between the sheets and, hearing Sylvia sobbing in the other room, squeezed her eyes shut. The thudding of her heart made her head ache. This whole business was crazy. She needed to leave for both their sakes. What she probably ought to do was talk to a lawyer.

It was Jimmy's brainstorm that Peg and Lauren meet at his house. He even apologized for not thinking of it earlier.

"You sure?" Peg asked over the phone at the office later that week. "What if Sylvia finds out?" But Sylvia usually worked late on Thursday nights.

"I'll claim to be innocently ignorant. Just kidding. How would she find out?"

"I don't know how she finds anything out, but she does. She should have been a private detective."

"Lauren wants you to meet her at my house after work today. I won't be home until late." He laughed softly in her ear. "It's better than doing it in the woods."

So Lauren had told him about their meetings at secluded parks, where they fulfilled their desperate need for each other against trees and on the hard ground while keeping an eye out for passersby. She laughed too — a harsh, dry sound.

Parking her car in Jimmy's driveway, she imagined Sylvia seeing it there. The garage door opened, and Lauren motioned her inside, next to her truck. The garage was unattached and they went into the house through the side door.

She followed Lauren upstairs to a corner room with two large windows and white walls at the rear of the house where they fell on a bed with a dark green bedspread and, wrestling off each other's clothing, hurried through the act of love. Lying apart and breathless afterward, she wondered at herself.

"Do you think there's something wrong with us?" Peg asked, staring at the high, white ceiling. A myriad of tiny cracks spread patterns across its surface. "Can't we talk before we do it?"

Lauren, who was lying naked next to her, smiled sadly. "I was thinking that myself." When she turned on her side, her breasts fell one on top of the other.

Peg never could resist touching them, and she traced the blue veins with a finger, then circled the aureoles as the nipples hardened. "I love your breasts." She bent to kiss them.

Lauren drew her into her arms and, rolling onto her back, placed her on top of her body. "We'll talk later." When their lips met, her toes reached Lauren's ankles.

They jumped apart when someone unlocked the side door and walked around downstairs, then climbed the steps. By the time footsteps sounded outside the bedroom door, they were sitting up frantically pulling on their clothes. The western sky bled, stained red by the setting sun.

"Sorry, girls. Don't mind me. Carry on. I'll be downstairs. My date canceled." They heard Jimmy rummaging around the room across the hall, probably changing clothes.

"What time is it, Lauren?" Peg asked, panic setting in. Hours had passed. The sun was setting. They had talked, made love, talked some more, made love again. How many times — three, four? Her lips were sore. "I've got to go."

"Why don't you eat first? Jimmy said there were leftovers that needed finishing." Lauren's mouth looked swollen.

Peg leaned over to kiss her and tasted sex. "It's too good, Lauren — the lovemaking."

"It can never be too good, Peg."

It was nearly nine when she left Lauren at Jimmy's. She drove home, fearing what she would find there. Sylvia's car was parked in the driveway. The light from the kitchen flooded a patch of yard. Letting herself into the house, she heard Sylvia talking on the phone. It took only a few horrified moments for her to realize who was on the other end of the line. She went to the kitchen doorway and stood there listening.

"Well, well, your little girl's home. Looks like she's been having oral sex."

Peg dove for the phone.

Sylvia held it out of reach and stared at the receiver, smiling a little. "She hung up. That was rude of your mother, don't you think?"

"Goddamn you. How could you?" She imagined her mother's outrage. She had never discussed her sexual orientation with her parents. At times she'd been tempted, especially in her youth when she was madly in love with her first woman. But she'd sensed that her mother didn't want to discuss Peg's sexual feelings or even admit that she had any. She'd have to call her, but she couldn't do it here.

Sylvia grinned humorlessly. "She has a right to know."

"You had no right to tell her." Galloping up the stairs, she grabbed the next day's work clothes and brushed past Sylvia toward the door.

Sylvia took hold of her. "Where are you going?"

"Let go of me, you fucking creep."

"You're not leaving." Sylvia tightened her grip. "I just wanted you to hurt as much as I do."

"You're too goddamn mean to hurt," Peg snarled. She jerked free and ran outside. Throwing the clothes into the Tempo, she slammed and locked the door.

Sylvia threw herself across the hood of the car and screamed, "Don't leave me. Please. Please. I'll kill myself."

Starting the engine, Peg put the car in reverse and began backing out of the driveway. Sylvia grasped the wipers and stared at her through the windshield with wide, frightened eyes. Peg slammed on the brakes, willing her to slide off. But Sylvia hung on, even when her body skidded across the smooth surface. The next-door neighbors appeared on their doorstep.

Placing her forehead against the steering wheel, Peg wept. Tomorrow she would call her mother and attempt some sort of explanation.

V

"Mom? About last night? I'm sorry." Peg sat in a deserted office. Noon on Friday was a lonely time at work. Everyone went out for lunch, which was good because for this call she needed privacy. She held her breath, awaiting her mother's reply. It was several moments coming and previewed with a deep sigh.

"All these years I've been pretending you're single because you were too independent to marry."

She waited for more. None came. "It's the way I am, Mom. I can't help it."

Another disturbing sigh. "But you can help who

you live with. I never understood what you saw in that woman." She sounded angry. "What on earth is the matter with her?"

Peg gave a soft scoffing laugh. "She's hurt. How's Dad?"

"So she wants to share it with me? As if I would sympathize with her?" Her mother's legendary Irish temper was rising. Born Maureen Carmody, she had named her daughter Pegeen after the Irish side of the family. "You know, Peggy, we haven't heard from you for weeks. It takes a call from that madwoman to get you to the phone."

"I'm coming home next Saturday if you'll have me." Father's Day was Sunday. She had planned to send a card, not take herself home, but now she had to mend fences. "What can I bring Dad?"

"Yourself." Her mother sounded somewhat mollified.

When she hung up, Peg wiped her forehead. It wasn't hot in the office — the air-conditioning was on — but she was sweating. She called Lauren, and listened to the phone ring. Surprised to find it was only twelve-fifteen, she drove to River Park.

During the past few weeks, she'd sunk into lethargy. Sitting on a park bench, she now noticed the evidence of summer unfolding. The trees thick with leaves still freshly green. The smell of cut grass sweetening the air. The river hurried northward, occasionally curling around itself, its water a molten sheet dancing in the glare of the sun. It carried mallards, gulls, and Canada geese on its thick current.

A battered green van towing a bass boat on a trailer swung through the parking lot and backed toward the boat ramp. When the trailer was hub deep in water, a man with a huge belly jumped out of the driver's side. "Git out here and help," he hollered.

A woman and two kids got out of the other side, slamming the doors shut. The man's door hung open. It was fringed with rust. The woman said something.

"Let one of the kids hang on to the rope. I'm getting in the boat." The man undid the nylon tie-down strap and released the hand winch. The boat floated off the trailer. "Hand me stuff."

The woman and boy carried a cooler, a couple of grocery bags, a tackle box, and fishing poles for the man to load in the craft. The girl held on to the rope. Then the woman parked the van and trailer, and she and the boy clambered into the boat. The girl flung the rope into the bow and hesitated, while the craft drifted beyond the reach of her short legs.

"You are so goddamn dumb," the man shouted, starting the engine and negotiating the bass boat back to the wooden pier jutting from the shoreline. When the girl jumped in, he cuffed her.

The scenario reminded Peg of the stories Sylvia told about her childhood. She had bought the tales lock, stock, and barrel. Now she wondered if there was only a glimmering of truth in Sylvia's claim that she had been abused by her father and older brother. And even if she had been misused, did that excuse her behavior forever? How old did a person have to get before she became accountable for things said and done?

* * * * *

Running the vacuum over the thick beige carpeting, Sylvia felt abandoned. Peg was gone this weekend to her parents' home in Cedarburg. She and Peg usually cleaned together. Aggrieved to be stuck with that chore more often than not lately, she thought it was as if Peg already had a leg out the door. She'd chop off the other one if Peg dared to put it out.

Tonight was the Women's Reading Group. The third Saturday of every month they met at the Green Garden Café, which closed its doors for the event. Two of the members, Jeanne Dobbs and Kathy Gordon, owned the restaurant. Deirdre was picking Sylvia up. The book for tonight's discussion was *Bastard out of Carolina.* She had been unable to read it in its entirety.

She debated calling Deirdre and telling her to forget it, but she dreaded a Saturday evening home alone. Turning off the vacuum, she put on the CD player and, dusting to the sounds of Lucie Blue, sang along with her. She fancied herself on stage in concert, using the dust rag as a microphone.

When the house was clean, she took a shower and dressed in cotton slacks and a short-sleeved cotton sweater. The red highlights in her hair glistened. She leaned toward the mirror, liking the way her nearly black eyes glowed with intensity. Shading her eyelids with beige eye shadow and her eyelashes with black mascara, she straightened and smiled at herself, then applied lipstick. Her skin resembled porcelain. No one would guess her forty-eight years.

She pictured Peg leaving the house that morning and had to admit she liked the way Peg wore her hair now — permed and long in the back, clipped short on the top and the sides. But the dull blue of her eyes, surrounded by dark flesh and sallow skin, gave an overall effect of illness. Peg's looks had once defined health.

She cast one last glance at herself and hurried downstairs as the doorbell rang. Motioning Deirdre inside, she grabbed her purse and the book by Dorothy Allison.

"Did you read it?"

"Not all of it. Did you?"

"I couldn't relate to the mother."

Sylvia frowned at Deirdre. "Of course you couldn't. You've never been a mother."

"My mother would have left that guy in a minute."

Irritated, she said, "Some women can't afford to tell their partners to shove off." Her own mother had stayed, no matter what her father had done or said. It had filled her with rage then as it did now. But she wouldn't admit it. "The book's not about your mother."

It was close to the longest day of the year. They went from the air-conditioning of Deirdre's Pontiac Sunbird to the artificially cooled café. Filling her plate at the salad bar, she sat at the long table made by pushing many smaller tables together.

Jeanne placed a hand on her shoulder. "Hey, how are you? You missed the last meeting, didn't you?"

"Sure did. You know why, don't you?" She looked Jeanne in the eye, her voice loud and clear. A hush fell.

"Would you like to talk?" Jeanne asked, motioning toward an unused corner table.

"Yeah, I would. But I don't care who hears. In fact, I want everyone to know what happened." She grew justifiably angry when she talked about Peg and Lauren.

Peg was having a real conversation with her mother. She wanted to ask why now after all these years her mother was allowing her to talk. Her mother had expressed shock over her appearance. Perhaps when she'd been here on Mother's Day, her sleep deprivation, her weight loss, her depression hadn't been so apparent. She stared out the kitchen window at her brother and father examining a tree in the backyard. "Something wrong with that oak?" Her brother doctored trees for a living.

"It's got some kind of wilt." Her mother's nearly black hair was flecked with gray, lending her a dignified appearance. Her eyes were green. She looked wonderful, vibrant.

"You like having Dad home?" Her father had retired in March, and Deb wondered if he took care of the gardening, because her mother still worked at the library. They were gazing out the kitchen window at the flowers in the yard. Her mother loved flowers and birds. Her perennials attracted hummingbirds. She put out oranges for the orioles. In the winter the yard came alive with birds flying to and from the feeders.

Her mother waved away the question. "I'm worried about you, Peg."

"Don't be. I'll get through this." But she wondered how. She was exhausted from the sleepless nights, driven to the edge by Sylvia's angry attacks, worried over Lauren's beginning impatience. She wanted to throw herself onto her mother's lap and become a child again.

"Maybe you should see a doctor."

"Sylvia wants us to go to counseling." The words popped out of her mouth; she would have taken them back. They'd been foremost in her thoughts.

Her mother rose out of her chair in agitation. "I don't see how that would help."

Neither did Peg, but before she could reply her father and brother came into the room through the patio door. As her brother aged, his resemblance to their father increased. Her father was bald, her brother balding. They had nicely shaped heads, though, and square jaws and straight white teeth. As if to make up for the lack of head hair, copious amounts of body hair sprouted from their torsos. Both were large boned and fit.

"I want to show you something, honey," her father said to her mother.

Her mother gave one of her sighs. "All right, Roger."

Her brother sat down and zeroed in on her as she watched their parents in the yard. "What gives, Peggy? You look like shit on a stick."

"Thanks, Michael. I needed to hear that." She wanted to cry.

"Dad said you had a falling out with Sylvia."

66

She turned her head sharply to look at him. "Did he say why?"

"No. What happened?" Her brother's large hands rested on the table. They were stained and hardened.

He would never understand. There was no point telling him. He was married, the father of three children. She shook her head.

"Ellen filed for divorce. I haven't told the folks yet." He gave her an indecipherable smile.

"Why did she do that?" she asked, surprised and instantly concerned.

"I guess I'm not exciting enough. She's in love with another man." He looked her in the eyes. "Your turn."

"I'm in love with someone else. Sylvia caught us together," she said, surprising herself. They had never exchanged confidences. "I'm sorry about Ellen."

"It's okay." He turned his hands over and picked at one of the calluses. "She never forgave me for cheating on her a few years ago. That was a mistake." His blue-black eyes, so like her own, pinned her in place. "But I don't blame you for wanting out."

They were talking as if her lesbianism was an established fact between them. "You all know then —" She couldn't finish the sentence.

He nodded and shrugged. Then he grinned at her. "I don't know about Mom and Dad, but I guessed long ago. You were always such a jock."

"There are women athletes who aren't."

"Sure there are, but they don't act like they're in love with their best girlfriends."

So that was how they knew. And she thought

she'd been so careful. She laughed aloud, before growing serious. "What about the kids?"

He looked pained. "We'll let them choose who they want to live with. They're old enough."

Michael announced his impending divorce after dinner. She should have been grateful that his news eclipsed her difficulties with Sylvia. Instead, she was vaguely put out and only later realized why. The demise of her relationship with Sylvia was regarded as insubstantial when compared to the end of Michael's marriage.

On the drive home, she was buoyed by the knowledge that not only did her family know she was a lesbian, they supported her leaving Sylvia. In fact, they couldn't understand why she continued to live with her. She decided to look in earnest for an apartment. It sounded easy enough. Robb would help and Jimmy; maybe Lisa would come back for the move. Who else could she ask? Not their joint friends or Lauren. She wouldn't subject them to Sylvia's anger.

She hoped that Sylvia would be gone, but her car sat in the driveway. Parking next to it, she took a deep breath and carried her overnight bag into the house and up to her spare bedroom. She was unpacking when Sylvia entered the room.

Sylvia was still upset from last night. Those stupid women. None of them could explain why the mother in *Bastard out of Carolina* had chosen the stepfather over her daughter. Someone had said her dependency was stronger than her love for her daughter. By that time she was ready to strangle them all. She'd told them. "She loved her daughter enough to leave her with an aunt."

"Dysfunctional, that's what they were. Ten to one the kid grows up and does the same thing. It's the abandonment fear and dependency rolled into one package," Kathy Gordon had said.

She would have stomped out of the café if Deirdre hadn't been driving.

When Peg turned as if sensing her presence, she said, "So, how was the weekend with your mama? Did you tell her about you and fat ass?"

Peg's eyes darkened nearly black. "You're always ready with an insult, aren't you? Always putting down people you don't like. My mother doesn't understand what I saw in you in the first place."

"Well, I always did say Maureen's snoot is so high in the air she doesn't know what's going on down here."

Peg took a step toward her. "Leave my mother out of this." She finished emptying her bag of dirty clothes. Changing into shorts, she said, "I'm going to read the paper."

Sylvia followed Peg to the back porch. A soft breeze circulated through the open windows, yet they were shaded from the hot sun. In the winter, the sun rode low enough in the afternoon to warm this room. Plants hung from the window frames.

Peg sat down and opened the *Post-Crescent* classifieds to APARTMENTS FOR RENT.

"Why are you looking at that section?" Sylvia stood in the doorway, pulling nervously on her fingers.

Peg glanced up over the paper. "I'm moving out, Sylvia."

"Let's go to counseling. Give us a chance." She knelt at Peg's feet.

"There is no us," Peg said bluntly, looking alarmed.

"Wait until we settle. Please."

"When is that going to happen? Get up, Sylvia."

Sylvia's knees were stiffening. Goddamn it. She got to her feet with difficulty, pain fueling her anger. "If you move out, you'll never get a thing. And I'll tell your boss."

"Go ahead."

"I saw a woman student leaving Lauren's apartment. Deirdre saw her too." It was a shot in the dark, a lie she hoped Deirdre wouldn't have to back up.

"I don't believe you. And how do you know she was a student anyway? If she was, Lauren was probably helping her with her work."

"I'll plant the seed of doubt. That's all it takes." Desperately searching for a way to hold Peg, she changed direction. "Remember how it used to be between us?"

"Yeah. You were either putting me down or you were losing your temper."

"We spent hours talking, discussing. Have you forgotten?"

"Guess so." But for a moment Peg looked thoughtful as if she did recall. Then she snapped the pages wide. "Look, if you won't let me read the paper, I'm going to leave."

"The grass needs mowing."

"All right, I'll do it." Peg marked a few ads with a pen and stuffed that page into her shorts as she got up, muttering, "Thank God for Mondays."

As Peg brushed past her, Sylvia thought she heard her whisper, "Lauren has a lovely ass."

Fury shook her. "What did you say?"

"Nothing."

* * * * *

1993

Lauren's quiet crying tore at Peg's conscience. She should let her go, tell her to get on with her life. Or she should leave Sylvia. She didn't understand what the affair was all about or she'd resolve it in some way. At first she'd thought it was as simple as lust, but quickly realized that wasn't so.

She and Lauren had developed a bond quite unlike the one she had with Sylvia. Peg crept around Sylvia's moods, accommodating her. Their relationship had never been honest, much less open, because she could seldom tell Sylvia what was on her mind. Her responses to Sylvia always aimed at pleasing her, at not stirring her temper.

But she and Lauren discussed everything and anything, sometimes picking up the threads of conversations for further exploration days later. She never hesitated to tell Lauren her thoughts, mentally storing them to share with her when they were

71

together. Their intimacy could not be defined as only physical.

Sylvia was out of town today. They lay in Lauren's bed, blanketed by the afternoon sun, the only sound Lauren's muffled crying. She found intensely disturbing the occasions when Lauren pressed her to make a choice, but she hated more this apathetic sobbing.

"Lauren, don't. Please." She began a soothing caress, thinking that might help. She loved the softness of Lauren's skin, the yielding firmness of flesh attached to the generous framework that held her together. Deriving great comfort from her breasts, so large and pliant, she always lingered over them.

A slight moan catching the end of a sob announced the beginning of passion. Lauren made an effort to turn.

"Lie still. Let me please you." Testing the heat between Lauren's legs, she found her wet all the way through. Working her fingers through the tangled hair, she penetrated easily.

Lauren again reached for her.

"Uh uh, not yet," Peg whispered. She was moving herself, her legs wrapped around one of Lauren's.

With a sudden show of strength Lauren put her on her back and, looking down at her, gave a throaty laugh. "You are such a pushover."

Lauren's husky voice set Peg shivering. Closing her eyes she pictured the large, capable hands caressing her intimately, the long fingers sliding in and out.

When Lauren went down on her, guttural sounds climbed her throat. Wrapping her arms around Lauren's hips, Peg pulled her close.

Lost in sensation, they moved together toward climax.

It was afterward that she realized passion only temporarily staved off the sadness, that Lauren wasn't alone in experiencing the emptiness of parting.

VI
1994

Sylvia was ushered into the office near the main entrance. The sign on the door read DEAN BEVERLY COMSTOCK, PH.D. She had told the dean on the phone that she wanted to help place students in job situations. Dr. Comstock had reminded her that this was a university center, that there were no graduating seniors. Sylvia had said that she had part-time jobs in mind.

As she took a seat across from the gray-haired

woman, Sylvia formulated her thoughts. There was a plate on the desk between them with the same information as on the door. How many pronouncements of her name and titles did this person need?

"What exactly did you have in mind, Ms. Everett?" Comstock asked.

Sylvia showed her best smile, in spite of her annoyance at this woman with her Ph.D. and her slight Southern drawl. "You may have heard of Everett Employment Agency?"

"Yes, you mentioned it in our phone conversation." The dean leaned forward and picked up a pencil.

Sylvia found her gaze drawn to the woman's heavy breasts, which brushed the desktop. They made her think of Lauren, and she felt her temper flare. "I wanted to help the students find employment to further their education. During my inquiries with several female students, it came to my attention that one of your faculty members has been abusing her position."

The dean raised a hand. "Wait a minute. You're going too fast for me. What inquiries?"

"I was doing a student job needs assessment."

"What students did you talk to?"

"I didn't ask for names. It was an informal poll." Comstock was making her nervous. She hadn't prepared herself for an inquisition. Where did the dean get off anyway? This was just an arm of the university; Comstock was small potatoes in the scheme of the state university system. "What I found out was that Lauren Platt, one of your faculty members, is using her position to seduce female students." Afraid the dean would interrupt, she hurried through the accusation and ended up breathless.

Dr. Comstock stared at her with a puzzled expression. "What on earth has that got to do with student jobs?" The woman stood up, a signal that the brief meeting was over.

"I thought you should know," she said. "It's important that this sort of thing doesn't get publicized." How dare Comstock show her out like this.

"I couldn't agree with you more. I hope it stays between the two of us." The dean didn't offer her hand. Instead she opened the door. "I will, of course, tell Lauren about our conversation."

"And the student employment situation?"

"I think that's your bailiwick, not mine. Feel free to post employment agency advertisements on the notice boards around campus."

On the way out, Sylvia took some flyers off the bulletin board and tacked her own business brochures in their place. When she turned and saw Lauren coming out of a room down the hall, a jolt of adrenaline shot through her. There were only the two of them in sight. She walked swiftly toward her.

Lauren froze in place. She looked thoughtful and spoke apologetically. "I've been wanting to tell you that I'm sorry." She shrugged helplessly and raised her eyebrows. "It happened."

"Shit happens and sorry doesn't cut it, cuntcakes. You messed up my life. If you were really sorry, you'd let go of Peg."

"She doesn't want me to let go, nor do I. What are you doing here anyway?"

"You might well ask." She heard her voice, low and sneering, vibrate with anger. "I just had an appointment with Dean Comstock."

"I'm going to see her right now." Lauren took a deep breath and their eyes met. Hers were a brilliant blue in the flush of her face.

When Lauren tried to walk past, Sylvia shoved her against the wall. "Whoops. I'm sorry too."

Lauren brushed herself off and continued down the hall, but Sylvia could tell she'd gotten to her. She hurried outside through the warm September day to her Volvo.

On the way to work she jumped a lane to get off the 441 bypass, and a car rammed her from behind. Hot, liquid fear coursed through her at the moment of impact. When they pulled off the exit ramp, she jumped out from behind the wheel ready for a confrontation.

"What the fuck did you do that for?" she asked the man who slammed the door of his green F-150 pickup. The left front turn signal was broken; the bumper and part of the left fender of the truck were crumpled. "Hitting my car couldn't have done that to your truck." Her vision blurred, then cleared.

"Where'd you learn to drive, lady? You must have been around before turn signals were invented."

A delivery truck that had passed them after the accident parked on the berm near the end of the exit ramp. A man got out and walked in their direction, the wind from passing cars whipping his pants legs. Then a squad car drove up behind the pickup. The officer swaggered toward them.

"Okay, what happened here?"

She looked at the rear end of the Volvo. The

right bumper was slightly dented; the side of that fender had a nasty bend in it. "Look at my car, officer. This man ran into me when I tried to exit 441."

The pickup driver jerked his ball cap off his head and rearranged it angrily. The blood vessels in his face darkened. "She turned right in front of me, no turn signal, no nothing."

By that time the delivery truck driver had reached them. "I was behind them both. I saw this lady jump from the middle lane to the exit lane without signaling. She rammed smack into the pickup. She'd been driving erratically, so I was watching her."

They were looking at her, waiting for her response. "I was driving like I always do. I was in front. I have the right of way. He ran into me."

"It doesn't sound that way, lady. I need to see a few driver's licenses. Why don't we just get in my squad car here, so we can get off the road?"

Half an hour later, Sylvia continued en route to the office. Despite her angry protests, the cop had charged her with causing an accident. He'd actually told her to shut up. She trembled in spite of the hot day. She wouldn't pay this ticket. She'd contest it until the cows came home.

Peg met Lauren at noon outside the art gallery on Morris Street. They sat on the park bench in the green space they thought of as their special spot.

"Sylvia told Dean Comstock today that I was

compromising my female students." Lauren spoke in a low, controlled tone.

Peg had seen enough of Lauren's anger to recognize it. "I'm sorry, Lauren. She's a vengeful person."

"I actually told her I was sorry for what happened. I've been waiting to say that to her face-to-face. God knows why."

"What did the dean say to you?"

"I offered to tell the whole story. She said that wasn't necessary, that she would take my word that I wasn't seducing my students. She wondered if Sylvia had all her cups in the cupboard."

"She said that?"

"No. She asked if Sylvia was mentally unstable. I told her she wanted revenge for something that had happened." Lauren gave her a wry smile. "Close enough to the truth."

"It is the truth." She looked into Lauren's eyes, searching for the thoughts behind them. Peg hadn't taken an apartment yet, although she'd been looking at rentals over two months now since the end of June. Dismayed by the cost, the small size of the units, the dark dreariness of so many of the buildings, she'd been unable to force herself to sign a lease. Actually, she was searching for one that didn't require an annual commitment.

"Well, she's played one of her trump cards and lost. You're next in line." Lauren met her gaze with a measured one of her own. "Are you ever going to move out, Peg?"

"As soon as I find a place."

"When's that going to be? You're looking for a

large, sunny apartment with no lease that rents for three hundred dollars a month. There is no such place, and you know it. Move in with me. If you can't do that, move in with Jimmy."

They'd had this same conversation over and over. "She'll never settle if I live with you. I'll call Jimmy." The decision, although she wasn't sure it was the right one, gave her a lift.

"You want me to tell him?" Lauren was grinning.

"I don't care. I'll have to talk to him anyway."

After leaving Jimmy a message on his machine, Peg drove home from work, determined to start boxing her things. As it always did, her energy deserted her when she got to the house. She dragged herself up the stairs with two boxes in tow and was greeted by moans and sobs coming from their bedroom where Sylvia lay in near hysteria.

"What's wrong?" she asked wearily after dropping the boxes in the room where she kept her clothes.

Between sobs Sylvia told her how she had been wrongly ticketed. "Goddamn men. They stick together like glue. They'll back each other's stories, no matter what lies they have to tell." By now she was convinced that she had signaled.

Peg knew Sylvia seldom used her turn lights, that she changed lanes without warning. She thought it a wonder that she hadn't caused an accident before now, but she said nothing.

Sylvia grabbed her hand. "Don't leave me, Peg. I was lying here thinking what it'd be like to come home to a house without you."

Peg snatched her hand back. "I told you I'd be gone if you said anything to Lauren's boss, and you did anyway."

"Please don't leave. I'll do anything." Sylvia was wailing.

"It's too late." What a relief it was to feel justified at last. She went across the hall and closed the door.

Sylvia leaped off the bed and shoved her way into the room with Peg. As fast as Peg filled the boxes, Sylvia emptied them.

"Cut it out." Close to tears, Peg sat back on her heels. How would she ever get out of here if she couldn't pack? She decided on the spot to gather enough clothes for a week and go to Jimmy's. She'd take vacation time and box when Sylvia was at work. Grabbing a couple of suitcases, she took clothing out of the closet. But when she put the clothes into the luggage, Sylvia removed them. She pushed her away. "Get out of here."

"You're not leaving." Sylvia clung to her.

"Let go of me." She slammed Sylvia into the door, then out in the hallway. They fell and wrestled on the braided rug they had bought together.

"You're hurting me."

Peg got up, her breath thick and hot in her throat. The evening was sultry with wet heat. "Good. Then stay out of my way."

"You're not going." Sylvia got up off her back. She rushed to the suitcases and threw the few remaining clothes in them into the closet.

Peg began to cry silently, hopelessly. "All right. I won't leave tonight." She would wait for Sylvia to sleep, then she would pack and get the hell out of here.

At two in the morning she crept around the bedroom, packing two suitcases in the dim light sifting inside, her heart pounding so loud she was sure Sylvia would hear it. When it came time to take the luggage down to her car, she could barely breathe through the din of her fear. She listened, knowing that the door to the bedroom where Sylvia slept was open, before carefully nudging the door wide enough to slip through. Amazingly, she managed to put the suitcases in the Tempo's trunk before the yard was flooded with light and Sylvia burst through the front door.

Peg jumped into her car, locked the door and turned the key with a shaking hand. As the engine caught life, she put the Tempo in reverse and swiftly backed out of the driveway. Then pulling the shift lever into drive, she sped away before Sylvia could reach the curb. Looking in the rearview mirror, she saw Sylvia running after her clad only in T-shirt and panties — mouth open and arms waving. As Peg neared the corner, outside lights illuminated neighboring lawns.

Pounding on Jimmy's side door, she saw his bedroom light overhead. "Hurry, open up," she muttered, sure that Sylvia was following.

They put her car in the garage next to his Ford Bronco, then carried her bags inside and up the stairs to the bedroom where she and Lauren had made love. This would be home now, she thought, trying to see it that way.

"Thanks, Jimmy. I thought I'd never get out of there."

He wore a short robe that failed to cover his skinny, hairy legs. His hair stood up in spikes as if he'd put a finger in an electric socket. One side of his face was creased and pink. "Want to talk or sleep? You look sort of beat."

"I am. I don't know if I can sleep, but I think I'll try."

"Good to have you here. Lauren will be pleased." He had one hand on the doorknob, ready to leave. "You know where the bathroom is. There are towels and washcloths in the hall closet next to it."

"I'll be fine. If you're up at six-thirty, will you wake me?"

Restlessly tossing throughout the remaining hours of the night, her eyes popped open at six. She wondered if she had slept at all, she'd been so wired when she climbed into the double bed. She showered and got ready for work before going downstairs to the kitchen.

"Toast?" Jimmy was dressed in suit and tie, looking trim and dapper. His eyebrows arched in unasked questions.

"Please." Sitting at the food bar, she thought she'd better choke down something. The nearly sleepless night was catching up with her. She was numb, her body leaden.

"Ask Lauren for dinner. We'll have a powwow tonight, sort of chew things over, decide where to go from here," he said.

She felt like a refugee, and tears burned her nose as she nodded and smiled her gratitude.

The neighbors closed in on Sylvia, asking if something was wrong, if they could help. She shook her head and waved them away, then retreated to the house where she called Deirdre.

"It's after two in the morning," Deirdre protested.

"I know what time it is," she cried. "Peg packed and left without a word, snuck out of here."

Deirdre sighed in her ear. "Maybe that's for the best."

"How can you say that to me?" She slammed down the phone, then snatched it up when it rang.

"Do you want me to come over?" Deirdre asked.

"No. She'll pay for hurting me like this."

"Let's talk about it tomorrow. Get some sleep."

"Who can sleep?" Her voice caught. "My heart is broken."

She went through the house, venting her rage on Peg's possessions. She'd teach Peg to walk out on her. As she deliberately ran the Swiss army knife that Peg had given her as a gift over Peg's furnishings, she felt the beating of her heart driving her. She set a newspaper ablaze on Peg's dry sink in the den, then put it out by pouring water over it.

The next morning she called a locksmith. He arrived before ten and installed deadbolts on all the outside doors. She wouldn't feel secure with Peg able to get in and out. And this way Peg would have to get her permission to move her things. Before she left for work, she turned off the electricity to the garage door opener.

"Morning, Sylvia," Judy greeted her, her young fresh face an irritant. "Here's a list of calls to return."

She glanced at the notepad, saw that Peg had not phoned. Grunting an acknowledgment, she went into her office and closed the door. Her wastebasket was overflowing with yesterday's paper. She marched to Judy's desk with it and was satisfied to see her secretary pale.

"I'm sorry. I was in such a hurry to get home last night I forgot to empty it."

She ought to fire Judy, she knew. Her work was sloppy at best, but she didn't want to deal with looking for a replacement. "Don't let your personal life interfere with your work, Judy."

"I fought with my boyfriend the night before last. I was anxious to make up."

"I don't want to hear it," she snapped. How unprofessional could the girl get? Returning to her office, she lifted the phone and put Judy out of mind.

When she left work around six, thinking it no longer mattered if she got home at a reasonable hour, she drove to the mall. She would buy herself something. It always made her feel better to shop.

The mall was nearly empty and she wandered from store to store, looking at furnishings. She wanted a lamp she had seen last fall, that Peg wouldn't buy with her. Now she knew why. Peg had been planning to leave even then. Anger rippled through her.

In one of the larger department stores she saw a

lead-shaded table lamp that resembled the one she had coveted. It would look good in the living room. "Excuse me, but is this the right price?" she asked a boyish looking salesman. The tag read one hundred and sixty-nine dollars. She thought that pricey.

He smiled and fingered the ticket. "Yes, ma'am. There's ten percent off on all furnishings this week, though."

She had him wrap and box it and carried the package out to her car. Tomorrow the Volvo was due at the body shop, which meant she'd have to rent one of their cars. They let one for ten dollars a day, but she thought they shouldn't charge. How could she leave her vehicle for repair without alternative transportation?

At home in the quiet house with only the refrigerator humming, she unboxed the lamp and put it on the end table next to the leather couch. Satisfied with the soft glow it cast through the pink shade, she went to the window and looked out at the park.

A man was walking his dog across the green grass. The temperature had been unusually warm, more like July than September. She pulled the draperies. Picking up the newspaper, she sat on the couch and stared at the glass doors covering the fireplace opening.

This is what it was going to be like without Peg. Lonely, empty, without purpose.

VII

The following evening Peg celebrated through a haze of fatigue. She could easily have fallen asleep. This was a relaxed weariness, not the edgy, draining exhaustion she'd experienced the past five months. Smiling sleepily at Jimmy and Lauren, she lifted her glass of Brut champagne and toasted her freedom. Tonight she would sleep with Lauren for the first time. Even when Sylvia had been out of town, she had not dared spend an entire night with Lauren.

"You escaped," Jimmy said. "I'm proud of you."

"Me too. Bravo." Lauren grinned ebulliently.

Peg smiled guardedly at their enthusiasm, knowing as she did that it was just a matter of time before Sylvia found her. "I need to get my stuff out of the house."

"We'll do that," Jimmy promised. "Tonight, though, is a new beginning. Let's forget yesterday and tomorrow for the moment. What do you say?"

That's why she liked him so much, Peg thought. He cared. "Okay." She looked around at the open windows, the closed side door. Was it locked? She wouldn't put it past Sylvia to cut a screen to gain entrance. She jumped when she felt Lauren's arm slip around her shoulders.

"What is it, Peg?"

"I guess I can't believe she won't show up in the doorway." When she'd least expected Sylvia, she'd appeared like an apparition.

"You look so tired. Let's eat and go to bed," Lauren said with concern.

"Not so quick." Slugging back his champagne, Jimmy refilled their glasses.

"We need to talk about what we'll do if she does come here," Peg insisted nervously, sure that someday Sylvia would do just that.

Jimmy looked from one to the other. "We've each got a key. We'll keep the doors and cars locked. No one will let her into the house for any reason."

"What about when someone's mowing the lawn or shoveling snow?" Lauren frowned.

"Lock the house, even if you go out for only a minute. You can always jump in your car and drive off." Jimmy made it sound like a viable solution.

God, she was tired. Her head spun as she slowly ate the potato salad and turkey ham sandwiches and salad Jimmy had provided. "Good food. Thanks, Jimmy."

"Tomorrow night it's your turn. I'll eat anything. One of my favorites is toasted peanut butter sandwiches with green olives."

When she and Lauren went to bed, Peg was apologetic. "I don't think I can make love tonight."

"Your first refusal," Lauren said with mock seriousness. She had propped herself up on an elbow. "I don't know if I can handle it."

"I hope I was worth the hassle," she murmured, thinking no one was. Yet she expected Lauren to say yes.

"So far, you are." Lauren lay back on her pillow. "Mind if I read? I'm apparently the only one who did get some sleep last night, being blissfully ignorant of what was going on."

"Lucky you." Peg shifted to her side, facing the window. The days were noticeably shorter. "Go ahead. Wake me if the house catches fire." If Sylvia set it ablaze. The thought momentarily alerted her while she considered the possibility and discarded it.

She awoke in the night, disoriented and sweating with fear from a rapidly fading dream. Moonlight had thrown a pale sheet across the bed. Lauren slept on her back covered by the ethereal light, breathing softly. Peg leaned forward to kiss Lauren's warm lips and eyelids, to caress the soft breasts and blow gently on the dark nipples showing through the ribbed cotton of her white undershirt.

Lauren stirred. "I thought you were too tired."

She lowered herself onto Lauren and heard her breathing quicken. "I'm wide awake now."

"So am I." Lauren's mouth was slightly open and

upturned in the shadowy recesses of her face, her hair a halo of curls in the moon glow.

"Sorry," Peg murmured, wrapping her legs around one of Lauren's, moving against it.

"Don't be. You can wake me anytime." Lauren responded with her own rhythm. Then turned them over.

Peg laughed, hearing herself deep and throaty. Why this particular woman excited her so much was a mystery. She couldn't pin down the attraction, and right now she didn't care.

They rolled from one side of the bed to the other, wrapped in an embrace, fingers teasing. Their soft moans became loud lustful groans, and Peg buried her face between Lauren's strong thighs, her fingers knuckle deep in a reservoir of passion. When she felt Lauren's arms around her hips, Lauren's tongue licking flames out of desire, Lauren's fingers probing, she became lost in sound and sensation.

Afterward, they lay quietly together until their thudding hearts slowed and their breathing normalized. The intense desire they elicited from each other always brought questions.

"It isn't just sex, is it?" Peg asked, her face in Lauren's neck.

"It's only your mind I love," Lauren replied. "Can't you tell?"

She could feel Lauren's breath hot against her ear. "Yeah, sure. What do you think it is? Really?" Their capacity for lust bothered her.

Lauren heaved a pleased sigh. "It's wonderful sex. Maybe that's the way it should be. I've never enjoyed lovemaking so much."

"Neither have I." Why feel guilt over something

so pleasurable, Peg asked herself. Why not instead be grateful?

When the weekend came, Sylvia began her search for Peg. She would talk her into returning home, but she had to find her to do that. She could barely stand the thought that Peg was gone, that she wouldn't be coming back. If she returned, she'd buy her new furnishings to replace the ones she'd damaged.

She'd placed a few calls to mutual friends, who claimed not to know where Peg was. When she'd asked them if they had any ideas where she might be, they'd demurred, saying they didn't want to guess. She crossed them off her list as obviously on Peg's side.

Parking around the corner from Lauren's flat with the front door in view, she turned off the engine. The day was cloudy and cool, a change from the warm, sunny days earlier in the week. Wouldn't you know the weather would turn when she had a day off and needed to spend it outside?

After a half-hour of eyeing Lauren's house, she decided she had to find a better way to locate Peg. She was too agitated to sit for long. To pass the time she called Deirdre on her car phone.

"I'm right around the corner from you, playing detective, watching for the fucking bimbo."

"What fucking bimbo?" Deirdre asked.

Deirdre could be so dense. "Lauren. Who else?"

"Oh. What will you do if she shows up?"

"If Peg's with her, I'll know where she's staying."

"And what will you do with that knowledge?" Deirdre said.

Sylvia was about to snap an answer when Deirdre invited her over for coffee. "All right," she agreed. She could always come back later.

Deirdre also lived in an older house in the area, but on the first floor. Her place was stuffed with furniture, the windows darkened with curtains, every available shelf covered with knickknacks. Sylvia followed her through the hall to the kitchen and sat at the table while Deirdre poured them both coffee and set out sweet rolls. She saw signs of Deirdre's cat, Ernestine, but not the animal itself who hid whenever she came over.

She put a piece of glazed cherry Danish on her plate and sipped her coffee, saying plaintively, "I just want to know where she is."

"Let her go, Sylvia. She isn't worth the hassle." Deirdre picked up her sweet roll and took a large bite out of it. Then she slurped her coffee.

What did Deirdre know anyway? She didn't have a lover, hadn't had one for years. "Will you ask around? See if someone knows where she is?"

"All right." Deirdre sighed.

"I need clothes to wear next week," Peg said Saturday morning over breakfast.

"Do you want to go to the house?" Jimmy asked, looking up from a plateful of pancakes.

"No," she said flatly, wishing she never had to go back.

"We should move you soon." Lauren was looking

at her, her blue eyes serious. She had spent the last few nights at Jimmy's, sleeping with Peg.

"I hate to think what that'll be like." Maybe she should just leave her stuff with Sylvia, but she couldn't afford to do that nor did she want to. She was very attached to some of her belongings — those with meaning, the things that had come down through her family or been given to her as gifts.

"It might be okay as long as Sylvia's not there." Jimmy looked doubtful.

"She'll find out. She'll be there." Her biggest fear, though, was that Sylvia would show up at work and make a scene. In spite of the conversation she took a few more pancakes and ate with relish. It was amazing how her appetite had returned. She was regaining lost weight. Out of sight, out of mind, she concluded.

Lauren got up to spoon more batter onto the griddle. It sizzled.

"What if she really does throw my things out of the house or give them away or something?" She knew how angry Sylvia must be.

"Well, honey, we can't do anything about it this weekend," Jimmy said. "You tell them at work Monday you need Tuesday off, and we'll move your stuff. Until then it's no use getting all upset."

Monday she asked for a vacation day, but had to wait until Wednesday to take it. She reserved a U-Haul truck, asking if she could pick it up along with a dozen furniture pads Tuesday evening. They needed to be ready to go early Wednesday morning as soon as Sylvia left for work.

Wednesday dawned sunny and cool, a perfect day to move. They showered, ate and drove to within a few blocks of the park. She and Lauren sat in the truck, waiting for Jimmy to scout the house and signal them that the area was clear of Sylvia

There were only the three of them. She couldn't ask Robb to help, because it would deplete their department. They were never allowed simultaneous vacations, nor had there been time to ask Lisa, and she didn't dare tell any of her and Sylvia's mutual friends for fear the news would leak out. She stared out the window, her heart flip-flopping nervously.

"How're you doing, sweetheart?" Lauren asked, reaching for her hand.

"I'm scared. I'm afraid she'll get wind of this and show up."

"You have to remain focused. Have you got the list?"

"Yes." She had listed her belongings and where they should be located. The truck was full of newspaper and boxes. How were they going to do this in one day? Some things would probably be left behind.

When Jimmy drove past and signaled for them to follow, she experienced breathing difficulties. Get a grip, she told herself. It was her chance to get out, and she'd better take it while she could.

As they parked in the empty driveway, she aimed her opener at the garage. When the double doors didn't move, she wasn't particularly surprised. Sometimes the switch was turned off. The three of them walked to the front door, and she put her key in the lock. When the door wouldn't budge, her gaze slid to the new lock above the old. Slightly alarmed, she went around to the backyard while Lauren and Jimmy unloaded boxes. The back door key slipped into the slot, but the new lock above it held the door shut. Sylvia had installed second locks, probably deadbolts. In a panic she hurried to Lauren and Jimmy with the news.

"We'll have to break in," Jimmy said without hesitation.

"Can we do that? I mean legally," she asked.

"A friend of mine broke into his place to get his stuff. You have a right to get into your own house." He was frowning. "Do you have any proof with you that this is your house?"

"I don't carry the deed around with me." How stupid she was. All the house papers were supposedly in the lockbox. She'd bet her last dollar that Sylvia had removed them. She stood in the sunshine feeling hysteria close in on her.

Lauren took her arm. "Come on, sweetheart. You can't do this."

"Let's go around to the back and break a window," Jimmy suggested, already walking in that direction, the other two trailing.

"I can't," Peg said, staring at the six glass panes in the upper half of the back door.

"Take this piece of wood," Jimmy said patiently, handing her a small round log he'd taken off the woodpile. "Then think of Sylvia and smash one of those panes."

She looked around furtively. "What if one of the neighbors sees and calls the police?"

"You do have a right to enter your own house," Lauren reminded her. "We don't have all day, Peg. Remember, we have a lot of stuff to box."

Taking a deep breath, Peg hit the pane. It didn't break. After three attempts, she lost her temper and rammed the log with full force. The glass shattered, tinkling down in small shards. Jimmy picked the pieces out of the frame and told her to wrap her arm in his jacket and reach inside to unlock the door.

Never had she broken a window, intentionally or otherwise. If the neighbors saw her, if one of them called Sylvia, if Sylvia returned, she couldn't allow herself to consider the possibilities.

They walked through the house toward the garage. The place looked strange to her as if she'd never lived here. Pausing to look around, glad that she'd already decided where and what to start boxing, she thought that this was a day that couldn't end soon enough.

Lauren and Jimmy went ahead to get boxes. They came back escorted by two policemen and Sylvia. Peg stared at them stupidly, her apprehension turning to shock.

Sylvia rushed to the back door. "See, what did I tell you. They broke the window. They're going to pay for this." Her voice rose in volume. "Arrest them."

Peg tried to sound indignant, but felt as if she'd done something wrong. "This is my house too. I'm trying to move out. She put in new locks."

"Wait a minute," an officer said. "Who are these people?" He was looking at Lauren and Jimmy.

"Thieves," Sylvia shouted.

"They're friends," Peg said, growing stronger in her resolve. She had a right to be here. "They're helping me move."

"Have you got any proof of ownership?" the other officer asked.

"My driver's license." She took it out of her wallet and handed it to him.

The two men studied her license, one looking over the other's shoulder. One of them looked boyish, the other middle-aged. The older one handed it back. "Why not let her get her things out?" he asked Sylvia.

"They should all be arrested for breaking and entering."

"Did you change the locks?" the young officer inquired.

"I knew she'd try to get in. I had deadbolts added. I didn't feel safe."

"You'll have to let her move."

"I'm going to swear out a warrant for their arrest," Sylvia shrieked.

Peg stepped back in the face of Sylvia's fury, knowing that Sylvia would never see another side other than her own.

"Lady, you can't keep her out of her own house." The older policeman looked and sounded annoyed.

Sylvia shoved Lauren toward the door. "Get them out of my house. She's fucking this woman. I don't want her in my home."

Lauren tried to break free. "Let go of me."

The younger officer separated Sylvia from Lauren, while the other said, "If you don't calm down, we'll have to take you in."

Shaking uncontrollably, Sylvia yelled, "Why take me in? They're the ones who are burglarizing my house."

"Where are the handcuffs?" The officer's jaw set in anger.

Sylvia visibly pulled herself together and pleaded, "Please, just let me watch to make sure they don't take what's mine."

Peg started in the bedroom, packing her personal effects and clothing. Wanting no mementos, she left behind the jewelry, artifacts, and pictures Sylvia had given her over the years. She did want the painting her parents had bought her for a housewarming present. It was an expensively framed, valuable original watercolor and was hanging in the living room. When she went to get it, she found the frame cracked and the glass scratched.

"What happened?" she asked Sylvia.

Sylvia shrugged and smiled. "How should I know?"

Peg went into the den in search of the dry sink she had bought at an auction. A burn blackened the inside. She hurried to the kitchen looking for the family dishes her mother had bequeathed her and found several with cracks in them. Fighting back angry tears, she glanced at her watch. It was late morning already. She decided then to take some of their joint possessions, something she hadn't been going to do.

Seeing Peg tag a chair and a lamp in the living room, Sylvia protested. "Oh no, she's not taking my things."

"They're mine too," Peg told the older policeman who stood nearby.

"Make a list, both of you, so you can keep track."

Sylvia followed her around, tearing the tags off as Peg put them on.

The officer said, "Lady, stop interfering. Go somewhere else."

Sylvia went toward the kitchen.

Peg heard Sylvia yell, "How dare you come into my house."

She ran to find Lauren kneeling awkwardly, momentarily unable to free herself from Sylvia, who was grasping a handful of curls and wrenching Lauren's head up and back. Peg lunged at Sylvia. "Let her go."

Sylvia turned on Peg in a flash and grabbed her by the throat. Tears streamed down her face. "You're taking everything from me."

Then Jimmy and the policemen were there, shouting. They pried Sylvia's fingers away from Peg's throat. Peg leaned against Lauren while the officers handcuffed Sylvia and took her, spitting angry words, out to the squad car.

The remainder of the afternoon went by in a disorganized effort to box and load the truck. Peg's concentration had been broken, splintered into different directions by the intense hatred of Sylvia's attack. She was shaken to the core, knowing that Sylvia had spitefully damaged her belongings. They were racing the clock now, having to unload and return the truck that night.

She went through the rooms, taking what she could find out of drawers and closets and cupboards. They loaded boxes first. Then they put into the truck the dry sink, her double bed and two oak dressers, the maple rocker and one of the living room chairs, several lamps and paintings, the walnut dining table and chairs, a tiled oak stand, three bookcases, a buffet and oak secretary that she had also bought at auction. The scratches and burns on the furniture sickened her. She thought they were meant for her.

They moved to the garage and quickly loaded her tools, her touring bike, her downhill and cross-country skis, her fishing rods and gear. The bike was stripped of accessories. The cross-country skis, which she had bought last winter, were scuffed and scratched. The bottoms of her downhill skis were crisscrossed with deep gouges. Her ski boots and bags had been slashed.

It was all she could do not to rush the squad car where Sylvia sat, kept there by one of the policemen leaning against the front fender. She knew it would give Sylvia great satisfaction to see her so upset.

Before they left with the truck, she made one last trip through the house. She searched the basement and attic, all the closets and drawers, the garage loft — knowing that she wouldn't be coming back, ever. There wouldn't be another chance for her to retrieve what was hers.

She pointed out to the policemen some of the damage done to her possessions. The two men murmured that they were sorry. She thanked them then and climbed into the truck with Lauren. Jimmy had gone ahead to make room for her things.

Disheartened, she realized that they would work into the night unloading, that she'd have to return the truck after hours and maybe pay extra rent. When Lauren leaned over and squeezed her hand, Peg felt resentment.

VIII

So Peg was living with Jimmy Jamison. Sylvia drove past the old farmhouse slowly, not caring whether anyone recognized her Volvo. Too bad her new car hadn't come in. She had ordered it soon after the accident, considering this one irreparably damaged, even though the Volvo had been impeccably repaired. She couldn't really afford a new car now that she was solely responsible for the house, but she didn't want anything to remind her of that unfortunate accident. She had even paid the fine rather than fight.

Peg's Tempo was parked in Jimmy's driveway, next to Lauren's pickup. Sylvia had futilely haunted Lauren's street. No wonder she hadn't seen Peg's car there. After Jimmy helped Peg move, she decided to look at his place.

She called Deirdre on her car phone. "Found her. She's staying at the faggot's house."

"It's six-fifteen," Deirdre moaned, "on a Saturday morning."

"Would you call her, Deirdre, and tell her I'm not doing so well?"

"But I thought you were better."

"I can't work, I can't sleep, I can't eat." She'd hoarded enough sleeping pills to do herself in.

"Please don't ask me to do that. I'll come stay with you if you want."

"Go back to sleep, Deirdre. I thought you were my friend." She clicked off. A wasted call. She cruised around the block, wondering if she should knock on Jimmy's door, then decided against it.

Parking a block away, she paged through the phone book she carried in her car before punching in Jimmy's number. The phone rang five times before the answering machine kicked in, and she hung up. Might as well go to work for a few hours and get something done.

Peg heard the ringing phone, heard the murmur of Jimmy's taped voice and the click of the hang up. She'd had trouble sleeping, knowing that Sylvia had outwitted her at every turn and wondering where she would strike next. She had forgotten to look for the house papers or receipts, and she'd been right about the lockbox being emptied. She didn't know how she would file taxes with so little information. Nor how she would get her fair share out of the house. Perhaps it had been precipitous to move out.

Lauren moaned and rolled toward her, throwing a heavy arm across her midriff. She smacked her lips a couple times in sleep and snorted softly. Her eyes moved under her closed lids, her lips fluttered soundlessly, her hands twitched on top of the covers. Was she too having disquieting dreams?

Sylvia marched through Peg's sleep, taking away the things Peg most treasured. Of course, in her dreams those possessions were always odd — a ball, a doll, the food off her plate, a bag of popcorn, a torn wall poster.

She looked at the clock. Had it been Sylvia calling? Had she found her? Who else would phone so early in the morning? There was no point in lying here, getting stiff and sore. Sometimes the bed became an enemy, hurting her bones and skin. She eased herself out from under the covers and pulled on sweats.

Water dripped through coffee grounds in the kitchen where Jimmy straddled a stool at the breakfast bar. He wore a torn gray sweatshirt and baggy jeans. His hair stood every which way, and he ran a palm over it when she entered the room. It sprayed back into its former shape as his hand released it.

"The phone wake you up, honey?" he asked.

She nodded. "Did you catch who it was?"

"Nope. I didn't even try." He smiled. "Coffee's almost done."

Sitting across from him, she met his eyes. They were the color of his hair, a nondescript brown. His face was pale, almost gaunt. "What's on the agenda for today?"

"Who knows? I seldom plan my weekends. What did you have in mind?" He raised unruly eyebrows.

"I lie in bed and wonder what to do about the house." she confessed.

He got up to pour the coffee. "I think you need to call an attorney."

"I did yesterday. This isn't the same as a divorce. I found that out. I don't have the same rights. No judge is going to see that I get half of our joint possessions, not even the house."

"But it's half yours."

She gave a bitter laugh. "Yeah, whether I want it or not. There's no written contract between us. Don't ever buy a house without a partnership agreement."

"Can't you haul her ass into court?" He set hot coffee in front of her.

"I engaged this lawyer. Maybe she can do something." She didn't want to think about it anymore. She was becoming obsessed with the house.

Lauren padded into the kitchen on bare feet. Her curls were tousled, her cheeks flushed, her eyes sleepy. "The honeymoon's over. There was a time when Peg would have lustfully attacked me before getting out of bed."

Peg watched Lauren pour herself coffee and refill their cups. "I didn't want to wake you. You were dreaming and snoring."

Jimmy laughed. "I believe it."

Lauren looked sheepish. "Sorry. I drove you away."

"That wasn't it. I kept thinking about the mess I'm in. I can't live here forever."

"Why not?" Jimmy asked. "I think we make one happy family."

"My furniture is stuffed into the spare bedrooms. How can you even have guests?" Was she looking for reassurance?

"I think Lauren should move in too."

Lauren snorted. "You just got me out, and you want me back? Besides, I've been here every night since Peg moved in."

"It's lonesome in this big house alone."

"Must I pay half the mortgage when I can't get into the house?"

Lauren and Jimmy looked at her. She was a step behind them, her thoughts never far from her own predicament.

Jimmy took her hand. "Honey, I don't think you should pay diddly-squat. Two can play her game."

"What game?" Peg asked, puzzled.

"Holdout. I told you about this friend whose lover locked him out of the house and wouldn't settle, just kept everything. My friend broke into the house once a month until his ex agreed to buy him out."

Could she shatter a window periodically? She looked at Lauren, who was shaking her head.

"I think you should stay away and let the attorney handle things," Lauren said. "How about some breakfast? I'll fix it."

The phone rang. Jimmy picked it up and after a few words, held it out to her. "Peg, speaking of the devil, it's Sylvia."

"I don't want to talk to her." She slid off the stool, a fierce rage coming over her.

Lauren squeezed her. "Good."

Peg pulled away. It was easy for Lauren to be so casual about all this. Her house wasn't being held for ransom, her belongings hadn't been sabotaged.

Sylvia called repeatedly, until the only response was the answering machine with Jimmy's request to leave a message. She left several replies, each one sounding at least as reasonable as the one before it. Lures meant to hook Peg. How could she resist the bait?

"If you want to talk about settling, give me a call —" "I'll buy the house. Let's decide on price —" "I guess you're not interested in dividing up the assets or you'd discuss it —"

Deirdre showed up at Sylvia's door toward evening. They were supposed to attend a hayride and potluck. Sylvia wished she were going with Peg instead. Hayrides in October were romantic events. Deirdre made her feel anything but amorous.

"I've been calling Peg all day. She won't talk to me." She was ready to explode from frustration.

Deirdre sighed. "Why do you bother with her?"

She thrust the phone at Deirdre. "I asked you to call her and tell her I'm not doing well. Why won't you do it?"

"You're better off without her."

"I'm not. I miss her terribly." Her voice caught on a high note.

Deirdre grabbed the phone. "What's the number?" She punched it in and listened to the echoing rings, then spoke to Jimmy's answering machine, leaving her name and number and asking Peg to return the call tomorrow morning. She handed the receiver back to Sylvia. "There. I've done it. Are you satisfied?"

"Tell her how much I miss her, that I need her and don't want to live without her." She smiled at Deirdre, feeling warm toward her. Peg would come back when she knew how much she was losing.

"Let's go. We're going to be late."

They met the others at the Green Garden Café. From there they carpooled to a farm just outside of town, where a wagon and tractor were waiting to pull them through pastures lit by the stars and a half moon. The night was warm for October with a soft, almost summerlike breeze.

Sylvia had brought a bottle of peach brandy with her. She passed it around with paper cups. "It'll keep you warm," she said.

Jeanne and Kathy, both recovering alcoholics, were sitting next to her and Deirdre. They declined and passed it on with murmurs.

"What?" she asked, knowing they were hard-nosed when it came to drinking.

"I thought there was going to be no liquor at these get-togethers," Kathy said.

Sylvia snapped, "You don't have to drink it. No one's twisting your arm. I need something strong about now." The wagon creaked and jerked on the uneven ground. The tractor nearly drowned out their voices. She waited for them to ask what was wrong, but neither did. They obviously didn't care. She shrugged.

The night was made for couples cozying up. She was ready to go to a warm place long before they made the return trip to the barn. The shakes set in on the drive to the café, and she secreted another slug of the brandy. Her mind was a pleasant fuzzy place, registering impressions.

She started to cry when filling her plate. The tears surprised her, but she gave herself over to them without a struggle. With a thud she sat down and howled, barely noticing that everything came to a halt.

Deirdre rushed over. "It'll be okay, Sylvia."

"It's not okay," she wailed. "Your lover's not fucking around on you."

Jeanne Dobbs put an arm around her. "Cry. Go ahead. It'll make you feel better."

"Nothing will make me feel better. She moved out. How am I supposed to go on alone?"

"I'm alone," Deirdre pointed out.

"You don't know what you're missing," she sobbed, tired of Deirdre comparing her situation to hers and Peg's. They were nothing alike.

She caught two words of what Kathy Gordon said: ". . . treat . . . better."

"What, Kathy?"

"She didn't mean anything," Jeanne reassured her.

"Yes, I did." Kathy stood up. "We should all treat our lovers better. Then maybe there wouldn't be so many breakups."

Wounded, Sylvia lashed out. "Are you saying I didn't treat Peg well? What do you know about our relationship? Huh? Nothing, that's what. I begged her to stay. I loved her." She got up. "Take me home, Deirdre."

"But we haven't eaten yet," Deirdre protested, her square jaw hanging.

"You can come back." She grabbed her jacket and

jerked it on. "You're an angry person," she told
Kathy.

"Oh, for Christ's sake," Kathy muttered with a
shrug. "There's no reasoning with you."

Sylvia pointed a shaking finger at Kathy. "You
insult me when I'm all torn up. You'd better treat
Jeanne better, or your heart will break too."

The three of them sat in Jimmy's Bronco outside
the Green Garden Café. They tried to peer through
the windows into the restaurant. Peg thought she
recognized Deirdre's Sunbird parked in the lot.

"I think we should go somewhere else," she said
just before Deirdre and Sylvia came out the front
door and walked to the Pontiac.

Peg held her breath and sank down with Lauren
in the backseat, whispering, "Does she know your
car, Jimmy?"

Jimmy slid down below the dash. "I hope not," he
said in a hoarse, low voice.

"Let's get out of here before she recognizes
someone."

As Jimmy started the engine and pulled away
from the curb, Peg saw the women milling around
inside. "It's women's night. I'm glad we didn't go
inside." It galled her to realize that she and Lauren
were effectively ostracized. To avoid meeting up with
Sylvia they stayed away from functions she, at least,
had once attended.

Sylvia had looked unsteady, leaning on Deirdre for
support. Peg felt relief that she wasn't going home
with her. But no one drank liquor at the women's

gatherings. Maybe Sylvia was sick. The messages she'd left on Jimmy's machine had almost gotten her to phone. Jimmy and Lauren had dissuaded her. Her attorney, Hannah Alexander, had said that Sylvia would hear from her in writing next week. She'd wait.

Jimmy chauffeured them to the new Serbian restaurant downtown. They sat under some hanging spider plants by the windows. It was nearly nine, but they'd gone to an early movie. He ordered wine and raised his glass.

"To friendship among thieves." He grinned engagingly.

Lauren mocked in a high voice, "Arrest them."

Peg wasn't amused. "That's what Sylvia does best. Calls people names." Cunt, asshole, fuckhead, whatever came to mind. Then why did she take it personally when someone, especially Lauren, made fun of Sylvia? Because it made her look foolish for staying with her so long?

"Sorry." Lauren put her glass down. "She's easier to deal with if you make light of her behavior."

"I know." She did know.

Jimmy dropped them off at the house after dinner. He was going to hit the bars.

Peg was always ready for bed, hoping to bury her thoughts in sleep or sex or a good book. Sometimes nothing staved off the worry. What drove her crazy was knowing that Sylvia wouldn't hear anything she said. She would, instead, twist it around and throw it back at her.

Lying in bed that night, listening to Lauren sleep, Peg realized she should have looked up Sylvia's ex-lover before getting so involved. She should have paid more attention to how she'd felt when Sylvia first kissed her over seven years ago. The magnetic part had been missing, the necessary physical attraction that drew two people together, that made them a couple rather than friends.

The first time they'd made love, Sylvia had been needy. She had been competent, but the fire only flickered between them. It wasn't the blaze that Peg and Lauren created with flames that never quite went out.

* * * * *

Spring, 1987

"Tell me how you happened to start your own business?" Peg met Sylvia's intense black gaze. She admired her keen mind, her passionate convictions.

"I decided I didn't want to spend the rest of my life making money for someone else. So I took the plunge. I had experience in the field, working for Job Search." Sylvia cocked her head and smiled tenderly.

When the check was put on the restaurant table, Sylvia picked it up. "Dinner's on me. Will you come over for Irish coffee? I love talking to you."

Peg realized that Sylvia had carried the conversational load, which was okay. Peg had encouraged her to talk. She enjoyed listening. "Sure. I have to take you home anyway."

Sylvia owned a condominium near Highway 41. The complex was located on the shores of Little Lake Butte des Morts, but her unit was on the backside, facing a woods. The interior was decorated in shades of white. Outside, the strategically placed lamps that edged the lawns and lent illumination to the surrounding woods made her feel safer, she told Peg.

Using street lamps to light up woods went against Peg's grain. Natural habitat should look that way. She stood in front of the bay window staring at the trees. "Nice place." Must have cost Sylvia an arm and leg.

Sylvia came up behind her and put her hands on Peg's upper arms. "Thank you." She leaned forward and kissed Peg's cheek. "I like you very much."

Peg turned to face her. "I like you too." Sylvia was moving a little fast for her. Peg walked to the couch and sat down. "I don't know if I should have Irish coffee. Doesn't Kahlúa have caffeine in it?"

Sylvia brought wine instead and sat next to Peg, who asked, "Have you lived here long?"

"I bought this place so there'd be room for my last lover. Do you believe it? She never even told me she was leaving." Bitterness tinged her voice.

"When did that happen?"

"Just before I met you."

Peg herself was recovering from a broken heart. Her breakup had been stormy. Her lover had found someone else and moved to Green Bay to be with her. It hadn't been a surprise, though.

She told Sylvia about it. "It was hard letting go. It helps that she moved away. Seeing her with someone else would be difficult."

"Even now that you've met me?" Sylvia asked.

Startled, Peg said, "I just met you. We hardly know each other."

Sylvia moved closer and put her arm around Peg. "We can help each other. I'm looking for a relationship, someone to share my life with, my dreams."

"I thought I'd found that person."

"You've found her now. I could easily fall in love with you."

IX
1994

Sylvia put the mortgage payment form along with
the electric and gas bills for the last two months in a
brown envelope and sent them to Peg by mail,
hoping they would elicit a response. In the evenings
she paced from room to room, picking up things and
putting them down somewhere else, then moving
them back. She hadn't heard from Peg since she'd
moved out.

When she got home from work the first day in

November, darkness had already blotted out the cold sun. She brought in an envelope from Donaldson, Frazier & Jacobs. Tearing it open she drew out the letter dictated by Hannah Alexander and read it. Her heart performed acrobatics in her chest and the familiar pounding began inside her head. Goddamn Peg. She'd gone and hired an attorney.

She would call Peg at work and Robb and Peg's boss. She'd tell them Peg was a lesbian, that she slept around, that she wasn't paying her share of the bills, that she stole things from work — pencils, pens, paper, books. They'd never know the truth of it. This was long past due.

She threw the letter on the table, then found herself drawn to it. Sitting down, she reread it carefully. The attorney wanted to arrange a meeting with her and Peg to talk about renegotiating the mortgage and dividing the joint possessions. Alexander suggested three different dates this month. None of them suited her. Tomorrow she would engage her own attorney. She wasn't going to settle until Peg apologized for breaking into the house, until she paid for window repair. Actually, she wasn't going to agree to any settlement unless it was a good deal.

Phoning Deirdre, she listened to the ringing until the answering machine came on and she banged down the receiver. Deirdre was never home when she needed her.

Peg had received the mailed bills the day before. "Look at these." She held the contents of the envelope toward Lauren and Jimmy. They were standing in the kitchen, still in their coats, having just returned home from work.

"What is it?" Lauren asked, shaking her head at the candy Jimmy was offering her.

"Come on, indulge, it's Halloween. Eat, before the kids get it all." He looked at Peg and shut up, but not before popping a miniature Tootsie Roll in his mouth. He leaned toward Lauren, who took the envelope contents from Peg.

Irritated, she said, "She's not paying the bills. Those are the mortgage, gas, and electric statements for two months."

"They'll turn off the gas and electricity," Jimmy said with a shrug. "Let her learn the hard way."

"My name's on those bills too. My credit is at stake." Rage threatened to choke her.

"You're not going to pay them, are you?" Lauren looked at her searchingly. "She's the one living in the house. Let her be responsible." Lauren frowned.

"It's so easy for you, Lauren." Exasperated, Peg grabbed her mail. "I'm going to change clothes."

"But Peg, you can't let her control you." Lauren followed her up the stairs.

She turned at the top. "Look, Lauren, it's not your house or your credit. Maybe you wouldn't be so quick to give advice if they were." Ignoring the stunned expression on Lauren's face, she went on to the bedroom alone.

When she returned to the kitchen, only Jimmy was there. He too had changed clothes.

"Where's Lauren?" she asked.

"Gone, left. What'd you say to her?" He was fixing drinks without asking if she wanted one. She seldom drank during the week.

"I said some things I probably shouldn't have, like it's easy to give advice when you're not the one who's losing everything."

He set a glass in front of her. "Drink it, honey, because I'm going to give you a piece of my mind."

She was amused and wondered why what he had to say never angered her. Was it how he said it? She sipped the vodka and tonic. It was icy cold. "I'm waiting."

"Never take your frustration out on your friends." He looked very stern.

She couldn't help it. She laughed. "Good advice. I'll call Lauren and apologize."

"Maybe I've been around too much," Lauren said into the phone. "It's okay, Peg. I'm not in your shoes. You'll have to do what you think best. Besides, I'm neglecting my work. I'll stay here tonight."

"Is she coming back?" Jimmy asked.

"Not tonight." Peg felt bereft.

The front bell rang, "The little buggers are arriving." He grabbed the candy and hurried toward the door.

She searched through the refrigerator for leftovers.

Wednesday, November second, Peg was unsuspecting, even surprised, to hear Sylvia's voice on the phone at work. "What do you want?"

"I just talked to Robb and your boss. I told them who you are and what you've been doing. I think they should know they're working with a lesbian who sleeps around and who steals company property, don't you?"

Peg felt as if the breath had been kicked out of her. She sneaked an involuntary glance at Robb, who returned the look with a thumbs-up sign and a smile. Her face went hot. "I never take anything. You know that."

"No, I don't, fuckface. I remember all the things you used to bring home," Sylvia said, her voice sweet and insincere. "Why don't you come home? I'll call your boss and tell him I was mistaken."

Peg's fingers sweated on the receiver that she held tightly with both hands, afraid it might squirt out and release Sylvia's words. "How could you, Sylvia?"

"I told you I would." Her silky tone sent shivers up Peg's spine. "You should believe me."

Remembering the bills, Peg said, "I'm returning those statements to you. I made the house payment the last month I lived there and paid my share of the other bills." They had taken turns paying the mortgage.

Sylvia hung up and chortled. She could be *so* bad, and it felt so good. Robb had told her to "stuff it" before she'd finished talking. She'd gotten even, though, when she told him he didn't know his prick from his nose, that it was probably that long too. But Peg's boss, Dell Burton, had listened and asked her how she got her information. "Firsthand," she'd said.

Sylvia glanced up to see her secretary, Judy,

standing in the doorway. "Don't you knock anymore?"

"I did knock. There's someone waiting on line two." Judy stage whispered, "An attorney, Doug Zelinski."

"Good. I'm expecting his call," she snapped. Did the woman think she was in trouble or something?

"Ms. Everett, what can I do for you?"

Sylvia explained the problem. She told him that Peg had moved out, after breaking into the house. She said she would send him a list of the things Peg had taken. She finished by saying that Peg was not paying her share of the bills.

"If she owns half the house, why did she break in?" he asked.

"I put on deadbolts for safety."

"You can't lock her out of her own house," he said.

"She moved out. I don't want her coming in when I'm not there and stealing things. Her attorney sent me a letter. I need a lawyer to represent my rights."

His voice was gruff and deep. "I have to tell you that you don't have the same rights as a married couple. In a divorce the community property law ensures equal division of property, but two single people owning a house together who separate aren't entitled to the same protection under the law. It depends on the judge, how he or she views your relationship. He could regard it as a divorce, or not."

Meaning, maybe, that she could make out like a bandit. Who would care? "What exactly are you saying?"

"It's cheaper to agree on a settlement. Do you want to purchase her half of the house?"

"If the price is right." She didn't want Peg to have the money yet. She might use it to buy a house with Lauren.

"Get it appraised by someone who works with your present mortgage company. Then we'll make an offer. And send me a copy of the attorney's letter. I require a five-hundred-dollar retainer, by the way."

"I'll mail you a check." It irritated her to have to send good money after bad. Peg was the one who had left, who should fork out the money for an appraiser. She wasn't ready to settle yet. Peg would have to pay through the nose if she wanted out financially.

Peg was mortified. She could barely look at Robb and waited anxiously for Dell Burton's summons. At noon she went home to escape Robb's embarrassing concern.

She called her attorney, Hannah Alexander, and asked if she should pay the bills or return them to Sylvia as she had said she would. Talking about money made her want to weep. If this dragged on too long, it might break her financially. She didn't have the resources Sylvia had.

"We can include who owes what to whom in a house settlement. Have you contacted the billing companies?"

A sense of hopelessness gripped her. "Not yet."

When she hung up, she called the mortgage

company and tried to explain what had happened to a snotty-voiced man. Awash in humiliation when he said he would make a note of her call but that the mortgage company was not responsible for their mortgagees' personal difficulties, she could barely keep herself from snapping a nasty reply. The woman at the gas company sounded confused. The man who listened to her at the electric company was sympathetic and asked if she wanted her name off the account. She said yes. Why hadn't she thought to ask the gas company rep to remove her name? She reluctantly called again.

Jimmy found her sitting next to the phone. "I didn't know you came home for lunch, honey." He gave the back of her neck a friendly squeeze. "I forgot my gym bag. I'm going to the Y after work. Want to join me?"

"No, thanks." She put the statements Sylvia had sent her in another envelope.

"Going to send those back to her, huh? Good. I hope they turn off the lights and the heat."

Please, not the heat, she thought. The pipes would freeze when winter finally set in.

"Is Lauren coming over tonight?" He started toward the stairs, looking back over his shoulder.

"I don't know." She wished she could shed the inertia that gripped her.

On her way back to work she flushed, thinking of Robb's efforts to reassure her. He had smiled, brought her coffee, patted her on the shoulder. She would have to ask about Sylvia's call, so that he could verbally offer his support and let it go.

Why hadn't Dell Burton called her to his office?

Was he as embarrassed as she was? Maybe he would discount the call. Perhaps Sylvia hadn't actually phoned him. She clung to that hope.

When summoned by Burton's secretary, she went with her heart in her throat and with no idea of what she would say. She'd been in his office before and thought it dreary — small with a window facing the parking lot across the street.

She found herself looking for her car out the window, avoiding his eyes. A furtive glance told her that he too was evading visual contact. When he cleared his throat, she tensed.

"Care to sit down." He gestured at the chair across from his desk.

With a mumbled thanks, she perched on the edge of the cushioned seat. She glanced at him and saw his nervousness.

"I had a strange call this morning from a Sylvia Everett," he began. "Do you know her?"

"Yes." Her voice caught and she added, "Unfortunately."

"She made some serious accusations that I thought you had a right to hear. I'm not giving them any credence, mind you."

She looked at him, her face fiery with shame. Her eyes burned. "I've never taken anything from work, not even pencils or pens."

"So, you know what she said?"

"She told me this morning that she'd called. She's a vindictive person when she's angry, and she's very angry with me."

He paused and took a deep breath. "I thought you should know. I didn't mean to cause you embarrassment."

"I've worked here fifteen years now," she started.

"Your job performance is not in question. Frankly, I thought she sounded a little deranged."

She heard the smile and glanced at him. "I'm sorry."

"Don't be." He stood up. "Forget it. I guess we can both get back to work now."

Robb looked over at her when she returned to her desk. Weak in the aftermath of relief, her face still hot, she managed a small smile. He must have taken it for encouragement, because he walked to her desk.

"Want some coffee?"

"Sylvia called you, too, didn't she?"

He nodded. "I told her to cram it. I didn't want to hear it."

"But she told you anyway. Right?"

"She got out a few words before I hung up. I never said this to you before, but she's an asshole and only other assholes would pay attention to that kind of talk." He grinned.

"She called Burton. He told me he didn't believe what she said. But even unmerited accusations plant seeds of doubt." She sighed heavily, remembering that Sylvia had said something similar.

"Ach," he said. "No one who knows you is going to believe her. Now do you want any coffee?"

"I'll pass, thanks." She'd have enough trouble sleeping tonight as it was.

Sylvia had wanted in the worst way to witness Peg's encounter with her boss regarding the accusations she had made. She'd played her trump card, now she was curious to know what havoc it had wreaked. Two days had passed, and she'd heard nothing.

Seated at the kitchen table Friday night, she put the mortgage, gas, and electric bills Peg had returned into a new envelope and sent them again to Peg's new address. If nothing else did, unpaid bills would get Peg's attention. Peg was scrupulous about making payments on time.

She had always regarded her as sort of an anomaly. Unfailingly honest, Peg never took money that wasn't her own. If someone undercharged her, she corrected them. Nor did Peg try to outsmart the IRS. Being totally honest on your taxes was stupid. The government wouldn't know if you padded your expense account, for instance.

Staring out the window at the streetlight, she recalled Peg's warning her: "You're going to get audited one of these days." That was something she could do, she thought. Tell the IRS Peg was cheating on her taxes. But she might have to give her name.

The phone rang. Deirdre said, "Want to go to a show or something?"

"Did you ever hear from Peg?"

"Not a word."

It made her glad that she'd called Peg's workplace. She put a stamp on the envelope. "Let's go out to eat first and then to a movie."

The week had been one long nightmare for Peg. Tonight she and Lauren were going to one of the local gay bars for Friday night fish with Jimmy and

Cal. She liked Cal, Jimmy's latest lover, but putting on a friendly face required an effort. Lauren and Jimmy entertained each other. She could watch from the sidelines and join in if she felt like it. Another person would force her into a show of good manners.

She changed into jeans and an old sweater. Because of the smoke, she'd have to throw whatever clothes she wore into the wash that night. Hearing Jimmy clamber up the stairs, she went into the hall.

"How're you doing, honey? Was it okay at work today?" Concern etched his face.

He'd been horrified when she'd told him about Sylvia's call to her boss and Robb. "She's a witch," he'd exclaimed. "She ought to be shunned."

"You're right." Lauren had chimed in pedantically, "The community ought to have nothing to do with people who use homophobia as a weapon against their own."

"I'm okay. How are you?" She'd gotten through the last six months, hadn't she? She could survive this bit of maligning.

"Just fine. Looking forward to this evening. Could I ask you something, Peggy?" He had taken to calling her that when he didn't call her honey.

"Anything, almost." She paused and watched him loosen his tie. He'd already shrugged out of his jacket.

"Maybe you and Lauren could stay at her place tonight. Would you mind terribly?" He looked worried and sounded apologetic. "It's just that Cal's never spent the night here. He might feel shy or something."

She laughed, surprised at the sound. "Sure. No problem."

In the bar they sat at a corner table and ordered drinks. Relaxing, she took Lauren's hand.

Lauren turned and smiled, her fingers tightening. The juke box was playing "The Power of Love."

"She knows how to belt out a song, doesn't she?" Cal said.

Over the sound of Celine Dion singing, "I am your lady, and you are my man —" she heard Sylvia's voice.

"There they are. Look at them — Mutt and Jeff, the sneak and the liar. Aren't they a cute couple?"

Deirdre was pulling on Sylvia's arm. Jerking free, Sylvia took a stool at the bar and faced Peg.

"Maybe we should go somewhere else," Deirdre said.

Sylvia patted the stool next to her. "Sit down, Deirdre."

"Oh god," Peg muttered. She refused to look at Sylvia. It was best to ignore her. All the tension was back. She was stiff with it.

"Want to leave, Peggy?" Jimmy asked.

Peg looked at Lauren, who raised her eyebrows and said, "Why should we go?"

Why indeed? Because she shrank from any contact with Sylvia? Because she hated public confrontations? Because she thought she might throw up? "My appetite's gone."

Jimmy went to the bar and whispered in the bartender's ear. He came back with an encouraging smile. "They'll toss her out if she doesn't behave."

Sylvia continued to stare at Peg.

"Can I get you a drink?" The bartender was standing behind Sylvia.

"Come on, Sylvia," Deirdre said, touching her arm.

Sylvia spoke without turning away. "I'll have a whiskey old-fashioned."

"We better order our food if we're going to the movie," Deirdre said. "Give me the perch dinner."

"I'll have the same." Sylvia spoke loudly, gesturing at Peg's table. "See those two women there. The short one used to be my lover. Can you imagine her cheating on me? With the bull dyke next to her?"

"Yeah, I sure can," Cal piped up. "If I could imagine women wanting women, I certainly wouldn't want you."

Nervous laughter rippled around them.

"You mealymouthed faggot." Sylvia started to slide off her stool.

The bartender, a tall handsome young man, reached across the bar and grabbed her arm. "Hey, any more of that and you're out of here."

Forcing a smile, she shook free and faced him. "Okay, pretty boy, you're the boss." Her tone was silken sweetness.

Peg felt hollow inside. She looked at Lauren and caught her shudder.

Jimmy smiled determinedly and put an arm around Cal. "You're a brave man."

X
1987

Peg was sick the month of November. So sick that she ended up temporarily moving in with Sylvia, who stayed home from work the last week of the month to take care of her. The sickness started as a cold, turned into flu, and finalized itself in pleurisy. She thought she was going to die. She would have gone home to her mother, but she didn't have the energy.

Sylvia fed her, comforted her, took her to the

emergency room, filled her prescriptions, brought cough medicine to her during the night, insisted that she adhere to bed rest as the doctor had advised.

As she recovered, a restlessness seized her. Feeling indebted for the long illness, Peg attempted to at least help with the household chores.

"I clean better alone, sweets," Sylvia said. "And you probably shouldn't fix dinner yet. Okay?"

"I'm better, Sylvia," Peg protested. "I'm ready to get up and do something, anything." Sudden coughing tore at her chest and left her gasping.

Sylvia hurried to get the cough medicine and poured a tablespoonful for Peg to swallow. "When you're all well, you can move in with me officially. I have room, and I love you."

"I love you too," she whispered, her breath rattling. But she didn't want to live in Sylvia's condominium. She would feel too vulnerable. As it was, she felt rushed into this relationship. Her friend Lisa kept telling her to back off, that Sylvia wasn't stable, pointing out how Sylvia jump-shifted moods.

Monday morning she dragged herself out of bed when Sylvia did.

"What are you doing?" Sylvia asked as Peg followed her to the bathroom.

"Going to work." She'd wear the clothes Sylvia had taken off her Friday ten days ago.

"You're sick, darling," Sylvia protested, jumping in and out of the shower in record time. Her auburn hair stood in kinky spikes.

Peg climbed into the tub and pulled the shower curtain shut. She felt terrible. Her head spun, her chest burned, and she was so weakened she shook. "I've had a week off. It's time to go back."

"I'll fix you some hot cereal," Sylvia called over her shoulder.

Leaning against the tile wall, Peg breathed in the steam rising from the hot water. She concentrated on the moment — showering, drying her hair, dressing, eating breakfast. The Cream of Wheat stoked her insides. "I'm going home tonight, Sylvia." She was no longer afraid to die alone.

Sylvia looked startled. "But why? Haven't I taken good care of you?"

"You have, and I'm grateful. But I need clothes for tomorrow's work." Just explaining made her break out in sweat.

"Get enough to wear for the week and come back. Please." Sylvia jumped to her feet and scraped her cereal down the disposal.

"Come on, Sylvia. I don't have the energy to fight."

"I spent days taking care of you, and this is how you thank me? You move out? Fuck you." Sylvia gripped the edge of the sink with shaking hands.

"What?" Stunned, Peg stared at Sylvia's back for a few moments. She got up slowly then and carried her bowl to the sink.

Sylvia turned and grasped Peg in a fierce embrace. "I'm sorry, darling. I just don't want you to leave. Come back as soon as you can. Okay?"

Peg stayed away until the next weekend. Somehow she got through the week. Robb brought her coffee, warmed up her car, proofed some of her work. She couldn't thank him enough, but he waved it away.

"You'd do the same for me," he said.

She would, she knew.

Lisa knocked at the apartment door on Wednesday night. "You look terrible, Peg."

"I'm better." It was true, and she gratefully sank back onto the couch. The disabling cough that caused such excruciating chest pain was under control. She told Lisa about Sylvia taking care of her and Robb doing all he could at work.

Lisa sat in the one easy chair. "There's something not quite right about that woman. I know you don't want to hear this. I lose friends by telling them what I think, but I can't keep my mouth shut. Don't move in with her, Peg."

"She's been good to me. Sure she has a quick temper, but she gets over it fast too."

* * * * *

1994

As November rolled over into December and Peg witnessed the painfully slow process of separating finances with Sylvia, she spent many difficult hours trying to sort out their relationship. How it had started, what she had wanted from Sylvia, why she had stayed with her so long after she saw her angry side. She no longer trusted her own judgment. Ashamed and defensive, she fought with Lauren whenever Lauren criticized Sylvia.

"She's codependent. Lots of people are," Lauren said one night when Sylvia came up in the conversation during dinner. Lauren wanted Peg to read *Codependent No More*.

"If I hear that word one more time, I think I'll scream." Peg glared at Lauren. "I suppose you think I was codependent."

Lauren glanced at Jimmy, who said, "Leave me out of this. I hate that term too."

"Well?" Peg insisted, her eyes boring into Lauren.

"You stayed with her, enabling her behavior." She spoke in a small voice as if reluctant.

Peg jumped to her feet. "It's so easy to label. When did you get your degree in psychology?"

"You're right." Lauren backed off, holding her hands palms up. "I've got no right to say those things. I want to understand why you were with her, is all."

"Look, if you don't love me enough as I am —"

"I do, I do love you," Lauren poured her soul into the declaration.

"What is this anyway? Soap opera time?" Jimmy looked up from his food. "We're enjoying a good dinner and you two have to spoil it. Sit down, Peg. If you two can't say anything uncontroversial, shut up."

Chagrined, they returned to eating.

When they were in bed, though, Lauren restarted the conversation. "I want to ask you something, but I won't if you're going to get mad."

"What?" She was too tired to be defensive.

"Promise?"

Curling up on her side away from Lauren, Peg said, "I'll try."

"Was your dad like Sylvia, or your mom?"

"What do you mean?" Through the window the clouded sky was tinted mauve by the city lights.

"Could you please them? Were they overly critical?"

"I don't remember it being hard to please them. What are you getting at?" Feeling Lauren's breasts press against her back, she tucked herself into the longer body. Lauren responded by encircling her with an arm and cupping her breast.

"I read that people sometimes unconsciously choose a partner who is like the parent they couldn't satisfy. Then they try to please the partner in ways they couldn't please the parent. The partner substitutes for the parent, duplicating an earlier scenario. People tend to repeat behaviors."

"I know that theory; I just don't understand it. Why, for instance, would anyone want to reconstruct an unpleasant parental relationship?" She leaned into Lauren's warmth.

"To resolve it, and because familiarity is comfortable."

"I've heard that too. But it's still hard to believe that people choose to repeat unhappy relationships because they're familiar. Don't they ever learn?"

"Were your parents verbally abusive?"

"God no." She turned all the way around and looked into Lauren's shadowed eyes. "They were good parents — kind, caring." Sometimes a little preoccupied, always busy, but whose parents weren't? She should take Lauren home to meet them. "I'll introduce you to them sometime." She rolled away again and folded herself into Lauren, adding, "They never liked Sylvia either."

Then she thought of something. "If people repeat

patterns, why did I choose you? You're not like Sylvia."

"I give up. You win."

Peg had returned the envelope unopened. Sylvia tossed it on the table. Her attorney had advised her to pay the mortgage and the other bills. If she hadn't already mailed him the five-hundred-dollar retainer, she would have fired him. He'd said she and Peg should divvy up when they settled. She had news for him. There was only one way she was willing to divide their assets. Peg didn't deserve anything. She'd betrayed their commitment. She guessed that Peg wasn't going to call her. To see her she'd have to agree to a meeting with the attorneys present.

It was December and pitch dark by five P.M. Her loneliness panicked her. What would she do for Christmas? She had no immediate family with whom she was connected. Even Deirdre had relatives to visit.

Slumping at the table, she buried her head in her arms. She couldn't stand the inner pain. Grabbing the phone, she called Deirdre. When she didn't answer, she phoned Jeanne Dobbs. It was Friday. The café would be serving; someone would be there.

When Jeanne answered, she wailed, "I'm so alone I could die."

"Sylvia?" Jeanne sounded alarmed. "Is that you?"

"Yes. Please help me."

"Why don't you have supper at the café? We have a good special tonight. We can talk later."

"Okay." Anything was better than staying home alone.

She took off her business suit, replacing it with a pair of jeans and a sweater. Getting into the Volvo, she paid only cursory attention to where she was going. A horn blasted her out of her reverie. Looking back, she realized she'd stopped at a red light, then gone straight ahead on a left-turn arrow. Easy enough to do. But it jolted her attention back on track.

Parking in the lot at the café, she hurried into its steamy heat. She hadn't been in the restaurant since the night of the hayride in October. "I'm here," she announced loudly, peeling off her scarf and jacket and hanging them on the coatrack.

"Find a table, Sylvia," Jeanne called, carrying a tray of food from the kitchen to waiting customers.

She looked around the room, rubbing her hands together to warm them. Her head snapped toward the windows at the sound of Deirdre's voice.

"Come sit with us, Sylvia."

Walking to the booth where Deirdre was seated with another woman, Sylvia was overcome with jealous envy. Deirdre hadn't told her she was going out with anyone. "I didn't know you were going out to dinner."

"It was sort of a spur of moment thing," Deirdre said. "Do you know Phyllis Newhouse?"

Sitting across from Phyllis, she felt a small surge of anger. Deirdre knew how desolate she was over the loss of Peg, yet she was waving a girlfriend in her face. She extended her hand. "I don't think so. Where did you two meet?"

"We work together. Phyllis is in the billing department."

"I've heard about you," Phyllis said. She had a husky voice that belied her small structure. Her eyes were hazel, her dark hair streaked with gray. She wore steel-rimmed glasses.

"Am I interrupting anything here?" Glancing at Deirdre, she saw the fleeting annoyance.

"We've already ordered," Deirdre said.

Jeanne was standing next to the table, pad and pencil in hand. "Are you hungry, Sylvia? The specials are eggplant parmesan and, of course, Friday night fish."

"The eggplant sounds good, Jeanne. Thanks for rescuing me." She gave Jeanne her warmest smile.

"What happened?" Deirdre asked.

She looked at Phyllis, pointedly ignoring Deirdre. "My lover left me. I've been so alone. Sometimes at night I think I'm going to die of loneliness."

"I've got news for you, Sylvia. You don't die, you just want to," Deirdre drawled.

She snapped, "How would you know?"

"You think I've never been lonely? I'm a little fed up with your sanctimonious sadness, as if you're the only one who's ever suffered a loss."

Where had that come from? She felt stabbed. "Why are you angry with me? I never did anything to you."

"I have feelings too, Sylvia. You could acknowledge them once in a while." Deirdre's eyes blazed.

"I lost my lover of seven years, and you think you know how I feel. When did that happen to you?"

136

"You had those seven years, Sylvia. Count your blessings."

Phyllis was holding Deirdre's hand as if to comfort or calm her.

Sylvia got up and looked around the room for another table. "I don't have to listen to this. You don't need me as a friend anymore, I guess."

Deirdre reached for her arm. "Sit down, Sylvia. I'm just tired of you taking me for granted."

Sylvia snatched her arm out of range, wondering what Phyllis saw in Deirdre. When upset Deirdre looked even more like a bulldog, her lower jaw jutting defensively.

"Fuck you," Sylvia said and noticed Kathy Gordon striding towards her.

"Come into the kitchen with me, Sylvia." Kathy took her arm firmly.

"What for?" But she lowered her voice.

"Just for a minute. Okay?" Kathy looked her in the eye, and she saw it was pointless to argue.

The kitchen was small and crowded and hot. She recognized the cook but couldn't place her by name. She didn't know the woman making salads at the long table. Kathy took her over near the back door, where the cold seeped onto her feet.

"You can't fight here." Kathy spoke quietly, flatly.

"I didn't start the argument. Talk to Deirdre." She was astonished. Tears filled her eyes. Her whole world was falling apart. She spotted Jeanne, coming in to pick up an order. "Jeanne, please talk to Kathy."

Jeanne looked at them. She made her way past the woman at the stove and the one at the

137

preparation table. "Sylvia, I know how unhappy you are, but we can't allow the other customers to be disturbed."

Sylvia was sobbing. "My coat's in the other room. I don't want to go out there."

"Look," Kathy said. "Why don't you stay in here, until you get hold of yourself. Then we'll set you up at a table in the other room."

Sylvia joined the woman making salads at the long table. "Can I help?"

The woman briefly looked up from her work. "It's not up to me."

Showing the woman a brilliant smile, knowing it shimmered through tears, she took an apron off the wall and washed her hands in the sink. "I always wanted to be a chef." She stretched a hand across the table. "I'm Sylvia Everett."

The woman wiped her hands on the apron that covered her jeans and T-shirt. "Julie Peterson." She looked out of huge brown eyes.

"How long have you been doing this?" she asked, taking over the job of ripping lettuce to shreds.

"Too long." Julie cut vegetables with amazing speed.

"You have wonderful eyes, so expressive." She could fall in love with those eyes.

Looking startled, then pleased, Julie warmed a bit. "I just do this in my spare time, to help out Jeanne and Kathy. I'm a beautician, looking for customers."

"I can't believe I haven't met you before."

Skinning an onion in record time, then half a dozen more, Julie said, "I moved here two months ago."

Captivated, she continued her questions, which

Julie readily answered. Sylvia forgot Deirdre's insulting behavior and Peg's betrayal. She asked if Julie wanted to go to a movie with her.

"Why not? Sure. We could take in a matinee this weekend. I have to work noons and evenings, though."

"Where are you living, Julie?"

"Upstairs here. I'm Jeanne's cousin on the maternal side." Julie grinned then, showing a wide gap between her front teeth.

Well, if nothing else, Sylvia needed new friends. That was obvious enough with Deirdre's defection. "I'll pick you up tomorrow after one. Okay?"

But the following day Julie had to be back at the café before five, so a movie was out. They went to the mall. Julie said she loved to shop.

Driving around the parking lot, looking for a vacant space that wasn't a half-mile away, she finally parked near Penney's. "You sure you want to go in there? It'll be a zoo."

"I don't mind."

Sylvia looked at Julie, ready to dump her and drive home. Obviously Julie didn't care whether she herself minded the crowds. But here was someone to make Peg jealous. If Julie kept her mouth shut, she could be classified as a knockout.

Resting her heels outside the dressing room while Julie tried on yet another outfit, she felt weary. When the younger woman emerged, she said, "I'm ready to leave." There were worse things than being alone.

"Where do you live?" Julie asked, once they were inside the Volvo. "I'd love to see your house. If it's anything like your car, it's got to be neat."

A sucker for such flattery, she showed Julie the house.

"You live here all alone?" Julie said, softening her up with wide chocolate-colored eyes.

"Since my partner left, I do," she said, dry voiced.

"I'd love to live here. If you ever want a roommate, let me know."

"I would never live with anyone who wasn't a lover," she said.

"I'd do your hair." Julie moved closer. "Would you let me style it for you?"

"Now?" She felt Julie's fingers in her hair, rearranging it. The touch felt wonderful.

"Next time." Julie glanced at her watch. "It's after four."

Sylvia felt a keen disappointment. "I'll take you back to the café."

XI

Nervous because she was meeting with Sylvia and her attorney, Peg sat with Hannah Alexander in the conference room at Donaldson, Frazier & Jacobs. Except for the long table and many chairs, the room was not unusual. The walls were papered, the floor carpeted. There were no windows.

She shifted in her chair, hoping that Sylvia would be in one of her more reasonable moods. Unable to rid herself of anxiety, she searched for something to say to Hannah, but every thought skipped away before she could hone in on it.

Hannah broke the short silence. "This is just a preliminary meeting to find some common ground." The attorney looked at the notes in front of her. "Apparently, the house was appraised. Let's hope it reflects fair market value. Then we can use it."

She zeroed in on that hope. "That would be nice." The pulse in her throat hammered wildly at the sound of Sylvia's strident voice in the outer rooms.

When Sylvia swept through the door with her attorney, she ignored Peg and reached for Hannah Alexander's hand. "I'm Sylvia Everett."

"Hannah and I know each other." Doug Zelinski shook Hannah's hand.

Sylvia said, "Mr. Zelinski, this is my ex-lover, Peg. The one who broke into the house and stole my things."

"Ms. Doyle," Zelinski said, smiling at Peg and shaking her hand.

Shamed and sullied by Sylvia's half-truths, Peg experienced a hopelessness that robbed her of resolve. She might as well give Sylvia what she wanted. She'd get it anyway.

"Let's review the situation here," Zelinski said.

He was a big man who gave the impression of boldness. Peg was afraid he would walk all over Hannah Alexander, a feminine woman if she ever saw one.

"She cheated on me, you know," Sylvia said suddenly. "I sold my condominium and bought a house with her in good faith. She betrayed the commitment."

Peg felt herself flushing. Knowing that everything she said would sound like an excuse, she decided against a rejoinder.

142

"We're here to work out a settlement, Ms. Everett. I hope we'll be able to do this in a reasonable manner that's financially advantageous to both of you," Alexander said calmly.

Sylvia bristled. "I'm not a child. I know what we're here for. She wants to take what's mine." She nodded at Peg contemptuously. "She already has."

"Ms. Everett, you're paying me to take care of your interests," Zelinski said in a soft voice. "Let me do it."

Dropping her gaze, Sylvia nodded abruptly.

"I have a list of things that Ms. Everett claims Ms. Doyle removed from the house." He handed a sheet to Alexander, who examined it and gave it to Peg.

Scanning the list, Peg was amazed at what was on it. Sylvia was claiming houseplants and Tupperware along with furniture and artifacts. She wanted to laugh. "Some of these things are not jointly owned. For instance, the dry sink. It's mine, and she deliberately burned it." She looked at Hannah, saw the slight frown. "Sorry."

Alexander handed Peg's list to Zelinski, who studied it.

Peg moved in her chair, shifting the anger welling up inside her. She had honestly listed their joint possessions, the few pieces she had taken and those she had left in the house.

Sylvia glanced at Peg's list. A ghost of a smile crossed her face as her eyes zipped down the page.

"Can we see the appraisal?" Alexander asked and took the paper that Zelinski handed her. She passed it on to Peg.

Peg was appalled. The house was appraised at one

143

hundred ten thousand dollars. They had paid one hundred thousand for it four and a half years ago. The market had boomed since then, and they'd made improvements — a new furnace, new carpeting throughout, a new roof with the skylights. She had sacrificed for this house, had gone without to buy it and to pay for the improvements.

She leaned over and whispered in Hannah's ear. "I can't go along with this."

"This appraisal is low for that house in that neighborhood. My client is willing to pay for her own appraisal."

"Then we'll have to meet again after it's done," Doug Zelinski said.

Sylvia's mouth worked angrily. "The bank recommended this appraiser."

"If Ms. Doyle wants a separate appraisal and is willing to pay for it, she can do that."

"I don't have to let anyone in my house."

"May I have a moment with my client?" Zelinski asked.

Peg and Hannah stepped out of the room. Peg breathed deeply, trying to dispel the anxiety that made even breathing difficult. She wanted to run.

Hannah smiled at her. "I understand now. You're right; she's not a reasonable woman."

Ashamed for Sylvia, humiliated by her, Peg wanted to melt into the wallpaper. How often had she wondered why she stayed with Sylvia, yet never made a move to leave? She and Lauren had to get caught in a compromising position, and even after that she had been pushed to the edge before she cut the ties with Sylvia.

Zelinski opened the door. "I've been fired. Why is

it I feel fortunate? Nice to see you again, Hannah. Good luck, Ms. Doyle." He nodded and was gone with a few pleasant words to the receptionist on his way out the door.

"Force the house to market," Peg said between set teeth as Sylvia passed her by without a glance. If she was going to lose her shirt, so was Sylvia. But she was desolate. She had counted on a settlement coming out of this meeting.

"Are you sure?" Hannah asked. "It's better to negotiate."

"And just how are we going to do that?" She swallowed rapidly, discouraging the tears that were burning her nose and throat.

Lauren was teaching an adult class that evening. Peg hoped that Jimmy would be home. She needed a sympathetic ear. Driving through the swiftly falling dark, she thought about her options. Should she keep trying to reach a settlement? With patience and time Sylvia might come around. Hannah was going to draft another letter to send to Sylvia, but without an attorney there was no one to ride herd on Sylvia's behavior, to set boundaries. She might even trash the house rather than pay a fair price.

Lights were on in Jimmy's house, and Cal's car was in the driveway. She slammed the Tempo door hard and made so much noise at the side door of the house that Jimmy flung it open.

"I hear you, I hear you. Nothing's going on, honey. Come in out of the cold."

The kitchen enveloped her in a warm welcome. She liked this room. Even though it was large, it exuded comfort. Only now did she realize that it was cold outside.

"Hey, Peg, how goes it?" Cal straddled one of the stools at the breakfast bar.

"Okay." She wished she were alone with Jimmy.

"Did you agree on a settlement?" Jimmy asked, helping her out of her coat.

"Are you kidding? Sylvia fired her lawyer because he told her I was entitled to a separate appraisal."

He looked shocked. "What a bitch. Now what?"

"Who knows?" She wanted a stiff drink. "I think right now we're at a dead end. And I took off work for this meeting."

Jimmy made her a vodka and tonic without asking and set it in front of her. "I don't understand why you can't make her put the house on the market."

"I'd have to obtain a court order, which would be expensive and time-consuming. My attorney is going to tell her we'll have to take that route unless she agrees to settle."

"Aren't there any laws that protect you?" Cal asked. Tall and thin and slightly stooped, he made up for what he lacked in looks by being quick-witted and kind.

Although she sometimes resented Cal's presence when she wanted Jimmy to herself, she thought the two men were a good match. "No. She wants the house, but she doesn't want to pay me what it's worth."

Enjoying a drink herself, Sylvia wanted to discuss the afternoon with someone. She hadn't talked to Deirdre since she'd seen her with Phyllis at the café

146

December second. Here it was the fifteenth already. Seeing Peg had stirred her up. It was the first year in seven that she wouldn't be shopping for her.

She phoned the café, but Julie was working in the kitchen. Leaving a message for her to call as soon as possible, she decided to give Deirdre a break and punched in her number.

"Deirdre? You busy?"

"Hi, Sylvia. Phyllis is here. What's up?"

No wonder Deirdre seldom called her anymore. "I fired my attorney today during a meeting with Peg and her lawyer."

"Why did you do that?"

"He told me I had to let her have the house appraised. I already had it done."

"So, are you going to get another attorney?"

"I don't know. Maybe I'll represent myself."

"That's always a mistake."

"What do you know about it?"

"I don't really, I guess. So, what's new?"

She told her about Julie.

"That's good. Maybe you'll forget Peg now."

"That'll be the day. I'm not done with her." She wasn't either. When she hung up, she called Peg, then slammed the receiver down when Jimmy answered and quickly punched in the number again. She could hardly believe her luck when Peg picked up.

"I want to talk with you alone," she said. She did.

"You're crazy," Peg replied.

"About you. This is foolish, this settlement stuff. Let's get together and work things out."

"Talk to my attorney." Peg hung up with a bang.

Sylvia stared at the phone. Rage flowed through her. She had bared her soul and Peg had rejected her. Tomorrow she would go to the Binery, where Peg worked. Peg would have to talk to her. Now she'd call Peg's mother and bring her up to date on her daughter. Someone should.

"Maureen, Sylvia here. I just thought I'd let you know that your daughter stole my possessions when she moved out. She's living with her new lesbian lover in Jimmy the fag's house."

The receiver crashed in her ear. That would teach Peg to hang up on her. She called Peg and left a message on the machine.

When she listened to the message, Peg knew she'd have to call her mother and apologize. She carried the portable phone to her room. She was pulling off her slacks when her mother came on the line. "Why didn't you answer? Why did you wait to hear my voice on the machine?"

"I thought you were Sylvia calling again," her mother said.

"I can't tell you how sorry I am, Mom. I wish I'd never met her."

"I wish you never had too. Are you safe, Peg?"

"I think so; I hope so."

"If she keeps bothering you, get a restraining order."

"How are you and Dad?"

"Better than you, I bet."

When she hung up, Peg went downstairs and ate leftovers with Jimmy and Cal. For some reason her appetite wasn't affected by all this. After dinner, she helped clean up and returned to her room.

"You don't have to disappear, you know. We're just going to watch TV," Jimmy said.

And neck shamelessly, she knew. "That's okay. I'm going to call Lauren later. I don't want to get involved in a television program."

Lying on the bed with her hands under her head, she stared at the ceiling. Her concentration was gone. Not even a good book held her attention for very long. Lauren was urging her to move into her flat. She had pointed out that there was no room for her things at Lauren's place. Lauren said they'd make room.

The phone woke her up. "Lauren?"

"How did it go today, sweetheart?"

They'd had to be so careful not to say something that would give them away during their affair that using endearments was only now becoming easy for them. She loved it when Lauren sweet-talked her. "Not good." She reviewed the afternoon and evening.

"What does this mean?" Lauren's voice was low, disappointed.

In her mind's eye Peg saw Lauren with her ear to the phone, stretched out on her bed. "Wish I were with you right now. Why didn't you come here after class?"

"I thought maybe you'd be waiting at my apartment when I got home."

"This was a bad day for me. I needed you."

"It's time for us to live together in our own place."

It was, she knew.

* * * * *

When the receptionist notified Peg that she had a caller, she thought it must be Jimmy or Lauren although she wasn't expecting anyone. It was ten minutes till noon, and she was going out to lunch with Robb and two other coworkers as they usually did on Friday.

She was so startled to see Sylvia that she stopped in her tracks. "What are you doing here?" she asked, her heart beating out of sync.

"Let's go to lunch. I want to talk," Sylvia said.

"I am going to lunch, but not with you." She briefly debated returning to her desk, but she didn't trust Sylvia not to follow.

Employees started trickling out the door behind her, and Peg was forced forward. The dribble turned into a stream, and she was propelled near the window with Sylvia.

"We can talk here," Sylvia suggested.

"No." She spied Robb in the flow of people and started toward him. If she could just reach him, he'd help her get away. "Robb," she called.

He turned his head and waited. "What's wrong?"

"Sylvia's here. Let's go to your car."

Taking her arm, he steered her out the door. She could see Sylvia following them. They walked quickly to his Taurus wagon. Both slipped inside, and Robb locked the doors. As they drove out of the parking lot, Sylvia pulled out behind them. She had parked curbside.

"She's behind us," Peg said.

"Do you want to go to the restaurant anyway or do you want to just drive around?"

"Won't Cindy and Ted be waiting?" Their coworkers.

"Probably not. They were supposed to go with us," Robb said, looking in the rearview mirror. "Tell you what, let's go to Taco Bell and order something where we don't have to get out of the car."

"I'm sorry, Robb." It pissed her off to be always apologizing to someone for Sylvia's behavior. "I don't even have my purse." It was locked in her desk.

"Hey, it's not your fault she's like this."

"It's my fault I was with her. I feel like such a fool."

"We'll eat in the car, and I'll let you off by the front door. You can't let her tail you, though."

"I know."

With the noon hour incident fresh in her mind, Peg phoned Hannah Alexander that afternoon. "Sylvia has called my mother more than once and said things that she has no right to say. She lied about me to my boss and threatened my friends." As she'd talked, her anger grew. "She's made embarrassing scenes in public places. Today she came to my workplace and harassed me. Then followed me in her car."

"Do you think you're in danger?" Hannah asked.

"Who knows what she'll do. She promised to destroy me. My mother suggested getting a restraining order against her."

"We can do that. If it's a case of domestic violence, the restraining order costs nothing. When it's sought to stop harassment, the charge is one hundred twenty-five dollars. We'll have to go to court to get it. You may have to answer some questions in court. You want me to go ahead?"

She said yes quickly, not allowing herself to soften. Her cheating was no longer relevant. Sylvia had more than paid her back. Besides, Sylvia should assume responsibility for her actions. When they had been lovers, she had tried to keep Sylvia within the realm of socially acceptable behavior. It was time to stop running around trying to catch the chips before they fell. If Sylvia's behavior was out of bounds, she should be nailed for it.

XII

In the kitchen at the café Friday evening, Sylvia invited Julie over the next morning. She said she wanted her hair done.

"Will you let me style it the way I want?" Julie asked.

"As long as it looks good." Maybe Peg would drive by and see another car at the house and wonder who was there.

"I should come over tonight. Wouldn't that be better?" Julie's hands rested on her hips as she grinned her gap-toothed smile.

She felt nothing for Julie except the need for another person in her life. It would be nice to have someone else in the house. "Do you want to spend the night?"

"Depends on where I sleep." Julie cocked her head, still grinning.

She wished Julie would close her mouth. "Wherever you want to." Smiling, too, because she realized Julie was after her body, her eyes slid down the younger woman, pausing at her breasts and hips. She had an enviable figure. If only Peg could see it.

Their initial efforts to please each other that night were disappointing. Neither was very wet, making sex difficult. Rummaging through the night table drawer next to the bed, Sylvia pulled out the vibrator and showed it to Julie. "It's ready to go. I just have to turn it on."

Julie's nose wrinkled. "I never use toys."

"Why not?" she asked. "They're useful." Sometimes they were necessary when one or the other bed partner couldn't come with the usual methods. "Come on. You'll like it."

"All right." Closing her eyes, Julie lay very still until the vibrator touched her. Her eyes popped open, then shut tightly. Her body quivered, her back arched, and she began to shake all over. "Oh, oh, oh," she said, the volume growing until she reached an explosive climax. After, she lay quietly again except for the tiny shivers that rippled through her.

A few moments passed before Sylvia realized that Julie had nothing further planned. She got up to pee and wash the vibrator. When she returned to the bed, the younger woman was asleep. She turned the vibrator on herself. The results were always spectacular, better than anyone could even come close to simulating.

When she wakened at first light the next morning, she pulled on sweats and went to the kitchen to make coffee. Retrieving the newspaper from the front steps, she read through it at the kitchen table with a mug of coffee at her elbow. It was her favorite time of day, and she completely forgot that Julie was upstairs in her bed.

"I'm sorry I fell asleep last night, Sylvia. I'm one of those people who can't stay awake once they hit the sheets. I'm a morning person. Let me take care of you now."

Looking up in surprise, she saw Julie framed in the doorway of the kitchen, dressed in an old bathrobe of Peg's that was too small. She frowned. "Where did you find that robe?"

"In the bedroom across the hall." Julie's disheveled hair and sleepy eyes were appealing, but then she stretched her sexy mouth into a smile.

"Why were you in Peg's room?" she snapped.

"I understand why you're angry. I'd be mad too, if you'd fallen asleep after I made love to you. I want to make up for it." Julie took a step toward her.

Sylvia looked at the bare feet protruding from under the robe with distaste. Why had she asked Julie to spend the night? "Do you want a cup of coffee?"

"I want you to come back to bed."

She spoke as if she were talking to a child. "I don't want to go back to bed. I want to read the paper and drink coffee. There are cups next to the coffee pot." The audacity of this young woman appalled her.

Julie shrugged. "Have it your way." She poured herself coffee and stared out the window at the park. "Do you want your hair done?"

"Later," she muttered, as she finished reading and slid the sections across the table toward Julie.

"I don't read the paper," Julie said.

She focused on the younger woman, wondering if she wanted this person disrupting her life. "What would you like for breakfast?"

"Whatever you want to fix. Not to have to cook is a treat." Julie pulled her chair up to the table.

The woman was a lead weight. Everything went one-way. "Hot cereal, toast, and orange juice. Then you can do my hair."

Looking at herself in the mirror after Julie left, Sylvia was unsure about the new styling. Her hair hugged her face in a twenties-vintage cap. She thrust her fingers into its perfection, tousling it, then brushed it smooth again.

Tonight Julie had promised her fireworks in bed. She wasn't sure she could accept the offer. Thinking about it made her tense. She'd put on a good show, acting as if she was looking forward to being on the receiving end of Julie's sexual prowess. In fact, she doubted if Julie knew half as much about pleasing her as Peg did, and Peg hadn't been able to make her come some of the time.

Peg and Lauren lay in bed, waiting for the sun to rise, hating to get up on a Saturday morning while it was dark. They were going to Lauren's today so that Lauren could work.

Debating as to whether she wanted to roll on top of Lauren and start something, Peg said, "Do you think our sex drive is diminishing?"

Lauren rested on an elbow. "I think we're more relaxed now that we can have each other whenever we want. We don't have to make frantic love as soon as there's an opportunity."

"You think I'm an easy lay, don't you?" she teased, as Lauren casually caressed her length.

"Are you?"

Shivering, she pulled Lauren down for a kiss. "Yes."

"Let's get up." Lauren released herself. "I've got a lot to do today."

Feeling vaguely insulted, she asked peevishly, "You don't want to make love?" Lauren had never backed off from lovemaking before.

"Maybe later." Swinging her legs over the side of the bed, Lauren sat up. "Brrr. These floors are always so cold."

"So are the floors in your flat," she snapped.

"I never said they weren't." Her fingers made peaks out of her already disheveled hair. "Something wrong, Peg?"

"No. Why?" She wrapped her arms around herself and rolled away. "I think I'll sleep in."

Walking around the bed, Lauren sat next to her. "I thought you were coming with me. What is it?"

Now thoroughly pissed at being turned down, even though she hadn't been motivated enough to make the first moves, she turned away again.

"We'll make love later," Lauren said. "Now come on, get up. I want to spend the day with you."

Taking enough clothes to last through Monday,

Peg left a note for Jimmy, who was asleep with Cal. They wouldn't be coming back that weekend.

Lauren fixed breakfast at her flat. Looking into the refrigerator, she bemoaned the fact that there was so little there. "It's all this sleeping around. We need to live together."

"So that the fridge is full?" But the fragmentation of their nights and days led to not knowing where to take the groceries. Should they stock two refrigerators? "I know what you mean, though."

Removing some milk, Lauren looked at her over the mouth of the plastic jug to which she was giving the sniff test. "When are you moving in?"

"Let's aim for March."

"That's three months away." Lauren set the milk on the table with a thud.

"The weather will be more predictable."

Later, while Lauren painted, Peg walked through the rooms and made note of where she would put her belongings. Lauren had said for her to decide, that she didn't care as long as she had room to work. She entered Lauren's workroom. "It's no fun doing this alone. You have to help."

"I will. Soon."

That was when she covered up with an afghan in the living room and buried herself in one of Susan Isaacs's books, *After All These Years.*

When she looked up to see Lauren standing before her, she realized that several hours had gone by. "What?" she asked. The room was cozy with winter sunlight streaking the floors and furniture.

"It's almost Christmas."

"I know. We need to talk about where we're going to be."

"I've always gone home to my parents Christmas Eve."

Peg stretched her legs, which had been folded under her. They were cramped. "Why don't we spend Christmas Eve together. You can go home Christmas day."

"Are you going to your parents?"

"For dinner probably." She and Sylvia used to go there together, because Sylvia had no close family. "You're welcome to come with me."

"If you come with me Christmas Eve, I'll go with you Christmas day," Lauren said, looking slightly alarmed.

"Have you ever taken a lover home?" she asked, curious.

Lauren shook her head. "I need to go shopping. I don't have any gifts."

"The mall will be shoulder to shoulder," she warned. For compensation, they could eat at Chi-Chi's Mexican Restaurante and drink margaritas.

By the time they reached the mall, it was four-thirty in the afternoon and dark. The parking lot by the theaters was actually clearing out, even though it was only thirteen days till Christmas. Peg'd purchased most of her presents at the beginning of the month.

She bought a box of caramel corn and sat on benches outside the stores while Lauren shopped. When they came to Waldenbooks, she closed up the box and went inside. "If I'm going home with you Christmas Eve, I'll have to have something to give your parents and whoever else is there."

Lauren looked panicked. "Let's not do it, Peg. Let's do what you suggested first. Spend Christmas

Eve together and go to our respective homes on Christmas."

Peg shrugged. It would be less of a hassle. "We'll think about it for next year then," she said, noticing Jeanne Dobbs browsing through the paperback fiction.

"Such a long time since I've seen you, Peg." Jeanne eyed Lauren.

"I think you know why," she said dryly. "Have you met Lauren Platt?"

"I've heard about you." Jeanne smiled.

"I bet you have. Probably nothing good either." Lauren grinned.

"Well, you know Sylvia. She's intense." Jeanne shrugged and laughed as if she'd told a joke.

"So, how're Kathy and the café? I wish we could eat there once in a while. But I don't want any more trouble." Even as she said it, she thought how unfair it was for her and Lauren. She wanted to ask if Sylvia spent much time at the café.

Jeanne's eyes darted back and forth between Lauren and her. "Busy. We've seen a lot of Sylvia. Actually, she's dating my cousin, Julie Peterson, who works at the café. I don't think you ever met my cousin. I tried to tell Julie what Sylvia's like, but you know how that goes. People have to learn on their own."

"Well, we'll stop by one of these days. Say hello to Kathy."

"I will. Nice to meet you, Lauren. And Peg, I just want to say that Kathy and I'd rather it was you hanging around."

It was a small compensation for voluntarily restricting her freedom to know that she was preferred over Sylvia, at least by Jeanne and Kathy. She moved off with Lauren.

Outside Dayton's, they ran into Deirdre and a woman she introduced as Phillis Newhouse.

Peg looked around, fearing that Sylvia would crop up. "So, how are you, Deirdre?"

Deirdre exchanged smiles with Phyllis. "Wonderful. And you?"

She marveled at the changed face of Sylvia's old friend. Deirdre would never be pretty, but happiness lent her a pleasant glow. "The same." She made small talk, having no wish to exchange information with Deirdre.

"I hope things work out for you, Peg."

Contentment had made Deirdre generous, she thought, and gave her a genuine smile. "For you too, Deirdre."

Lauren had made purchases along the way; together they were laden with them. As they passed Santa Land on their way into Dayton's, Lauren suggested they go have a drink.

At Chi-Chi's, the bar was crowded with former shoppers. Finding a small table, they ordered a pitcher of margaritas and loaded bowls with chips and salsa from the food bar. The Christmas music playing through the speakers was drowned out by a football game on TV.

"Feels good to sit down, doesn't it? But if you really want to go the café, I'll go with you," Lauren said.

"No, thanks. Sylvia's got a girlfriend. Maybe she'll leave us alone now."

"Does it bother you?"

She thought before she answered, searching herself inwardly for hidden feelings toward Sylvia and found nothing. That was odd, she thought. There should be some emotion, if only relief, but she couldn't dredge up any. "No. Perhaps she'll want to settle now, though."

Deirdre and Phyllis took what they called their table at the Green Garden Café. Coming out of the kitchen, Sylvia spotted them where she had first seen them together and went over to say hello. The many plants in the windows were draped with tiny, white lights. A Mexican wreath was hanging on the door.

"Want to join us?" Deirdre asked.

"Can't. I'm helping in the kitchen." Julie needed her.

"Guess who we saw at the mall."

With annoyance she said, "I suppose you saw Peg. I don't care about her anymore, Deirdre." But she had to ask anyway. "Was she alone?"

"No."

"How was Lauren-the-hun?" she asked, surprised by her own vehemence.

"She looks pretty much the same."

Phyllis added her unsolicited observation. "She seemed nice enough."

They both looked at her.

"You can't tell from a few words," Deirdre said.

"I don't agree. I liked her." Phyllis lifted her chin defiantly.

"Do you know what they did to me?" she asked, stung by what she considered a rebuke.

Phyllis met her eyes. Her voice faltered. "Yes."

"Phyllis," Deirdre began.

Shaken by the brief confrontation, Sylvia cut off Deirdre. "Never mind. I don't care what she thinks. What does she know." Hurrying back to the safety of the kitchen, she tore up lettuce and talked distractedly to Julie.

Driving home through the decorated streets, she felt fragile and alone even though Julie followed in her beat-up Honda Civic. Parking the Volvo, she unlocked the front door. The house welcomed her, soothing in its familiarity. Switching on lights, she closed the living room drapes.

Julie took off her jacket, threw herself on the couch, and patted the cushion next to her — for all the world as if she belonged there. "Take a load off, Sylvia."

"When I'm ready," she snapped. This was her house. She wished Julie would remember that. "Want a glass of wine?"

"Sure."

When she returned to the living room, it was dark except for the candles on the mantel that Julie had lit. Again she was offended by what she considered presumptuousness.

"I think candles are romantic, don't you?" Julie asked.

"As long as I don't fall over something." She struggled to keep her growing annoyance under wraps.

Julie, however, seemed unaware that anything was wrong. She toasted the two of them, then slipped an arm around her. "After we finish this, can we go to bed?"

When they stood face-to-face in the bedroom, Julie attempted to undress her. She'd never let anyone take her clothes off, not even Peg. She resisted when the sweater she was wearing cut off her vision and threatened to strangle her. "I'll do it." Folding her clothes neatly, she placed them on a chair, then slid between the sheets with Julie.

"Don't you ever abandon yourself to passion?" Julie asked, her brown eyes amused.

The question plucked at a sore spot. She remembered Peg saying, *They're my clothes. Just let them lie in a heap and come to bed. Tidy up after we make love.* She'd told Peg she didn't want to get up afterward, but that hadn't been the reason. She just couldn't leave things piled on the floor.

Instead of answering, she thrust her tongue down Julie's throat.

Julie drew back and wiped her mouth. "Let's start out dry. Okay? Where'd you learn to kiss like that?"

"You don't like the way I kiss. You obviously think I'm compulsive. Why are you here anyway?" Even to herself she sounded strident.

Pulling her close, Julie whispered, "Come on, shhh. Let's make love, not war."

She freed herself. "I can't make love with someone who does nothing but criticize me."

"I'm sorry," Julie said, lying back and putting her hands behind her head. "Do you want me to leave?"

"No." Sylvia turned on her side and ran a hand over Julie's voluptuous body. Her breasts were like twin mounds of risen bread, she thought. Her belly rose slightly above her hipbones. She slid testing fingers into the tangled crop of curls between Julie's legs. The silken skin was hot and wet. Leaning over, she suckled one of the large nipples while forcing two fingers deep inside.

Julie grunted and arched her back, and the fingers became engulfed in secretions.

Burying her face between Julie's breasts, she slowly pulled the fingers out and caressed the delicate genitalia. Then she took the other nipple into her mouth.

Knowing that she herself was wet, she allowed Julie to reach between her legs. The touch felt like fire, but when Julie tried to insert a finger she whispered, "No."

"Why not? I want you."

"Not yet." Rubbing against Julie's hand, she came in a matter of minutes.

"Now can I go inside?" Julie asked.

Sylvia grabbed Julie's arm. "I'm done. Let me finish you."

While Peg was driving home from Chi-Chi's, Lauren startled her by kissing her neck and fondling her breasts. "You ever do it in the car?" she asked as she teasingly rubbed a hand against the seam between the legs of Peg's jeans.

Peg protested the kisses, sure that others could see, but she moved toward the pressure of Lauren's hand. "Yes. Have you?" She held her breath as Lauren unzipped her jeans and slid a flat palm down her belly to cup her crotch.

Managing somehow to penetrate her, Lauren said, "Lift your hips."

"I'm driving. Can't we wait till we get home." As

desire gripped her, she thrust against Lauren's hand. But she didn't want to come this way. "I want your mouth."

Parking carelessly, grabbing their parcels out of the backseat, they galloped up the stairs to Lauren's flat. They dropped the bags on the floor inside the door. Shedding their clothes they made a trail into the bedroom — shoes first, then sweaters and jeans, socks and underwear.

Wrapped in each other's arms, they kissed, rolling over on the bed. Smacking their pleasure, laughing, talking in spurts, they reached between each other's legs. Lauren always ended up on top. The disparity in their heights made mutual oral sex possible only in this position.

XIII

Peg's holidays at her parents always whisked her into the past. She showed up late Christmas Eve as her brother was waving his kids off in his future ex-wife's car. The Tempo's lights swept over him, momentarily silhouetting his figure and upraised arm against a backdrop of snowy blue spruce trees draped with colored lights. It made her think of a Hallmark card gone awry, celebrating Christmas without the wife and kids.

He met her at the car door. "Glad you're here, Peggy."

"Were those your children leaving?" She embraced him as he nodded. "I'm sorry I missed them. Are you okay, Mike?"

"It's harder than I thought it would be," he said with a deep sigh as he took her luggage while she retrieved a bag of gifts from the backseat. He grabbed her arm when she slid on the fresh snow-covered drive. "We'll go down together. So, how is it with you? Mom said that Lauren is coming for dinner tomorrow."

"Yep. We've changed our plans three or four times now. This is a brave thing for her to do." She wanted Lauren to feel welcome.

"It'll be a quiet Christmas. I'm glad she's coming. Why aren't you with her tonight?"

Lauren hadn't asked her, that was why, and she hadn't pushed for an invitation. She'd spent the early part of the evening with Jimmy and Cal instead, celebrating with a steak dinner and wine. Lauren had explained that Christmas Eve at her parents' home was chaos with nieces and nephews running wild, that she would rather have her visit when there weren't so many people around.

Their parents waited in the library. Flames leapt in a fireplace flanked by book-filled shelves. The remaining walls were paneled with richly colored tongue and groove walnut boards. A Douglas fir, decorated with ornaments accumulated over many years, glowed with color in the corner windows farthest from the fire.

"We're toasting," her mother said after greeting her. She handed each of them a glass of champagne.

They did this every Christmas, every New Year,

every birthday. The toast was a silent one, like a prayer.

"Are you hungry, Peg?" her mother asked when she opened her eyes. "There are plenty of leftovers."

"I ate, thanks." Looking out from under her father's arm, she felt like a kid again. For a day or two, she would gladly let her parents take over the reins of her life.

They exchanged recent news for about an hour, until her parents went to bed. As they always had, they would open gifts in the morning. She stayed behind with Michael in the library. Her brother fed logs to the fire from the hinged wood box by the door to the garage. Brushing loose dirt off his hands, he sat on the couch next to her.

"I love this room," she said quietly.

"It's a sanctuary," he agreed. "My kids should be so lucky." He looked at her. "We were fortunate to grow up with both parents in a house like this."

"I'm sorry, Mike," she murmured.

"It's not your fault." He shrugged. "Did you ever want kids, Peggy?"

Had she? Staring at the pulsing fire, she thought about his question. "It's not uncommon for single women to have kids now. I guess I just dismissed the possibility, because I knew I was never going to marry. If I had it to do over, I think maybe I would have one child."

"You're not too old, Peg." His smile was so sad it made her ache.

"It would be hard." For one thing, she'd be closing on sixty when the child was twenty. And Lauren would have to agree to it.

"I miss my kids. I don't want them to have to choose between me and their mother, though. That's asking too much."

"Are you going to let her have primary custody?"

"Probably."

In bed in her old room the silence was so profound it was unnerving. She started when a great horned owl hooted from the yard. Another answered farther away. Getting up, she padded to the window to see the denizen of the night perched in the oak tree that suffered from wilt. The bird's large body and the tufts of feathers sprouting like ears from its round head gave it away.

Temperatures ranged in the single digits, and the lower halves of the windows were patterned with frost. The owl hooted again when she hurried back to the double bed where she had slept during her growing years. Sometimes friends had stayed the night. When that had happened during her teens, they'd used the dark as a mask. It had allowed them to experiment with sexuality. If you don't see it, it didn't happen.

When she woke the next morning, blinding sunlight was striking the frosted windowpanes, breaking the rays into patterns. Hating to get up from the warm bed, she snuggled under the covers until a full bladder forced her out.

She pulled on sweats and went to the john. After rinsing her face and brushing her teeth, she descended the stairs. Her parents waited in the kitchen for the water to finish dripping through the coffee grounds. Birds flashed to and from the feeders out back — bright colors against the snow. Michael was building a fire in the library fireplace. It could have been a Christmas morning from her youth with just the four of them. Realizing this scene was unusual so late in her life and might never be repeated without adding or subtracting someone, she stood in the doorway between the two rooms, soaking up the ambience while watching the birds and waiting for coffee.

When the doorbell rang around two in the afternoon, she'd been on edge with expectation and jumped to answer it. Pulling Lauren inside along with a rush of cold air, she gave her a furtive kiss. "Merry Christmas."

"I hope it's merrier here." Lauren shivered. "It's freezing out."

Looking into the familiar, loved face, she tried to read it. "Did you have a bad time?" Taking Lauren's coat, she hung it in the hall closet.

"Let's not talk about it now." Lauren looked around. "Nice place."

"What's in the bag?"

"A little something for your folks. Fatwood for fire starting."

"That's nice. Gird your loins, it's intro time." Propelling Lauren toward the library, she girded her own. When she introduced Lauren, she mentally stepped back and viewed everyone from a distance.

Her mother was small, straight-backed and elegant. Wearing dress slacks and a silk blouse, her dark hair swept behind her small ears, her green eyes set off by tasteful shadowing, she made a fashion statement out of simplicity.

Casually dressed in slacks and flannel shirts, her

171

father and brother stood side by side. They reminded her of large friendly dogs, nonjudgmental and eager to please.

Lauren was composed and pleasant. She had brushed her curls into a semblance of order before they left the foyer. Her blue eyes were bright, her cheeks ruddy from the biting cold. At five-ten, she made a commanding figure. She wore wool slacks and a midnight blue sweater that accentuated the color of her eyes.

Fixing dinner had always been a family affair with everyone in the kitchen contributing something. Lauren fit right in, helping wherever she could, sipping wine along with the others, joining the conversation. And by the time they sat down to eat, she had traveled inroads that Sylvia had never even got near in seven years.

In Peg's room Christmas night they whispered together after making careful, quiet love. Heedful of staining the sheets or making noise, they kept their panties on and their moaning under wraps.

She asked Lauren about her "merrier" remark that afternoon.

Lauren said, "I'm just glad you weren't there. My sister and her husband bickering over everything from money to the kids who ran wild. My brother doing the passive-aggressive thing by refusing to control his children. His wife becoming angry because he wouldn't stop watching a football game to help with anything. My mother getting frantic to have everything on the table on time. My father being so quiet I couldn't figure out what was wrong with him. My brother-in-law asking me if I'd met a man I liked yet. My sister telling me I didn't understand kids because I didn't have any. Etcetera, etcetera. Too many different people confined under one roof."

"I'm sure my parents think you're the cat's meow."

"In comparison to Sylvia, I hope so."

"Let's not get into Sylvia bashing. Okay?" She was immediately annoyed.

"Sorry. Did you tell your parents you're moving in with me?"

"Yes," she said, still a little peeved.

Lauren beamed at her, a flash of white teeth in the dark. "It's really going to happen, isn't it? I thought maybe it never would."

On the day after Christmas, Sylvia went to the office and cleaned up the paperwork on her desk. She had spent the day before with Julie at Jeanne and Kathy's café, where they had held a Christmas potluck. Deirdre and Phyllis had shown up for an hour, wearing gold bands on their left ring fingers, their presents to each other. Sylvia smarted with envy at their ecstatic happiness, which reminded her of her own discontent. Deirdre strutted a little too much.

Looking out the window at Highway 41, she wondered if Lauren had gone home with Peg this Christmas as Sylvia had done in the past. What a drag that had been. Peg's mother always so snooty, thinking she was better than others. Her father was okay, though, not too much of a chauvinist. Her brother was like her father, unassuming and friendly. But his wife was a witch and his kids were loud and disruptive. She was glad she hadn't had to go there this year. Now Lauren would be sucked into all that family stuff.

Julie had given her a gorgeous sweater and a camisole. The two presents had looked lonely, though, among the many gifts she had heaped on Julie: a leather jacket, wool slacks and a silk blouse, Jockey underwear, a sexy sleep shirt and bathrobe. She had spent hundreds, a ratio of four of her dollars to one of Julie's. But she told herself that Julie didn't have much money to spend. She remembered lavishing presents on Peg, too, and receiving little in return. Her eyes filled with tears, and she shook them away.

Tonight the café was closed and Julie would be over early. She had to leave work mid-afternoon and start dinner. They were having turkey tetrazzini and noodles. Locking up the office at three, she drove home.

Letting herself into the house, she hung up her coat and turned on the CD player. Lighting a fire in the fireplace, she poured herself a glass of wine and sat in front of the flickering flames until they took hold. She went upstairs around four-thirty, after starting dinner, and put on the camisole and sweater Julie had given her. Why did she always get the cheap lovers, she wondered. Maybe she was too generous.

As she came back downstairs, she noticed the dark through the skylight. Julie arrived, and Sylvia closed the door quickly behind her, shutting out the cold night.

"You're wearing the sweater I gave you," Julie said, her brown eyes softening. "Do you like it?"

174

"Of course. And you've got on the jacket and slacks, I see. Do you like the sweater and the undies and the bathrobe and nightshirt too? Are you wearing any of them?" She had to be careful not to snap.

Julie opened the jacket. "Yes. You know I love clothes. You were too generous."

"I always am," she observed wryly.

"I have the undies on too, and I brought the nightshirt and bathrobe with me," she said with a sudden grin.

"I guess I didn't waste my money." She was glad, though, that she hadn't purchased the gold necklace she had considered buying for Julie.

"What's wrong, Sylvia?" The brown eyes lost their glint.

"Nothing." She turned toward the kitchen.

"I don't have a lot of money to spend."

She waved away the excuse. "I know. It's okay." But she felt somehow devalued. "I'll pour you a glass of wine. We'll sit in front of the fire for a few minutes."

Sylvia had been served with the court papers. Peg knew that, because she'd paid to have it done. Yet neither Sylvia nor her attorney were in court. There was no opposition to the restraining order. Hannah Alexander was representing her, and Jimmy had come along to offer moral support and to testify if necessary. Lauren was teaching that afternoon.

She had obtained written statements regarding Sylvia's behavior from her mother and Lauren and

Robb. She hadn't wanted to ask her boss. Hannah Alexander presented them to the judge for her. And Peg was asked why she sought the restraining order.

"I want Sylvia Everett to stop harassing me and my relatives and friends. She has threatened to destroy me and has lied about me to my supervisor and coworker. She did the same thing to my friend, making false accusations about us to her dean. She calls my mother and upsets her with half-truths about me. " In anticipation of Sylvia's appearance, her heart beat overtime and her eyes darted nervously toward the coutroom door whenever it opened.

"Now honey, take a deep breath and calm down," Jimmy whispered in her ear at one point. "If she comes, I'll handle her."

When she left the courtroom with the two-year restraining order in hand, she was exhausted from the apprehension. "I hope I never see her again," she said. "Maybe her not being here means she's not going to bother about this anymore."

"If she does contact you, call the police," Hannah said, picking up her briefcase. "Show them the restraining order. Carry it with you."

"Congratulations, kiddo," Jimmy said. "I'll walk you to your car."

"Thanks for coming, Jimmy." They stood in the parking lot in the raw January day. Shredded clouds sped across the sky in front of strong winds.

"I have to go back to work for an hour, even if it is almost four o'clock." He opened the door of the Bronco, which was parked next to her Tempo. "Don't let her get to you, Peggy. She's not worth it."

"I know. See you later." She jumped into her car.

The Tempo rocked in the wind as she took the ramp onto 441. She was going to Jimmy's to get some clothes to take to Lauren's. The car behind her that had been climbing her frame drew alongside the Tempo as soon as the two northbound lanes were accessible.

The vehicle had looked vaguely familiar in the rearview mirror. Peg threw an annoyed glance at the driver and recognized Sylvia. Hot bile shot up her throat and she forced it down past the hammering pulse in her neck.

Sylvia gave her a wolfish grin.

Peg accelerated, but the Volvo stayed effortlessly by her side. Knowing she couldn't outrun the larger car, she slowed down and tried to ignore it. She wondered if it was her imagination or was it really edging closer, pushing her toward the berm. Glancing in her mirrors, she hoped someone would come along and want to pass. She took her foot off the gas and coasted to fifty. Maybe there would be a traffic cop in the median strip whom she could ask for help. For some reason, the Volvo and the Tempo were the only two northbound cars on the four-lane bypass.

As if reading her mind, Sylvia exited where Peg had planned to get off, so she now was forced to continue to 41 and backtrack. When she got to Jimmy's, she was so badly shaken she could barely unlock the door. Why did she let Sylvia unnerve her like this? She phoned the police, knowing she'd have to file a complaint and not wanting to take the time to do that.

She arrived at Lauren's late, around six-thirty, unhappy with the lost time. Letting herself into the flat, she found Lauren in the kitchen.

"How'd it go this afternoon?"

"I got the restraining order, and she broke it before they had time to serve it." She told Lauren what had happened. "There were no witnesses. It's her word against mine, but I reported her anyway. That's why I'm so late."

Lauren stood by the butcher-block table, her blue eyes alarmed. "You think she was trying to drive you off the road?"

"I don't know. It felt that way." Maybe that's why she'd been so scared. "It never ends, does it?"

Two uniformed policemen stood outside Sylvia's front door. "We have a complaint against you, Ms. Everett. Peg Doyle said you pursued her with your car this afternoon after she obtained a restraining order against you."

"She's a liar." Stupid of Peg to report something when there were no witnesses. "Do you want to come in out of the cold?"

They stepped into the foyer. "Where were you between four and five this afternoon?"

Where had she been? She thought quickly. "Grocery shopping."

"Where?"

"Mike's Super Plus." Actually, she'd been getting out of her car at Copps on Calumet when she'd spotted Peg climbing into hers with a sack of groceries. She had followed her, but there was no way they could prove anything.

"Once the restraining order is served, you're going to have to stay away from her. If you see her somewhere, don't talk to her and leave as soon as possible. If you break the restraining order, you're liable for arrest."

"I haven't broken anything," she snarled. "Goodnight, officers." She closed the door and locked it.

She was furious over the court business. Her newly hired attorney had told her not to challenge the restraining order, to stay away from Peg. *She* should ask for such an order, not Peg. She was the one who had been cheated on. She had a right to be angry, to let others know what Peg and Lauren had done to her.

Phoning the café she got Jeanne on the phone. "We're busy, Sylvia. I'll tell Julie to call you as soon as she's done working."

"The police just left. Peg's trying to get me arrested."

"Why don't you come over. Then you can talk to Julie while she works." Jeanne sounded impatient.

No one cared, she thought. She'd considered continuing on to the café after she'd left Peg on 441, but it was so nasty out that she'd gone home and built a roaring blaze in the fireplace. After banking the fire, she closed the glass doors. Maybe it would still have life when she got home.

Snow blew in a steady stream across the road in front of the Volvo, transferring drifts from one side to the other. It made her shiver to drive through the windy night. Parking in the lot, she hurried inside the café.

The place was packed for some reason. Why anyone wanted to go out to eat on such a horrid night was a mystery to her. She walked through to the kitchen, where Julie was putting together salads. No longer did she want to be a chef or a short-order cook or a sous-chef. Too much pressure and too much repetition.

Julie looked up from the carrots she was dicing. "What's this I hear about the cops bothering you?"

"Peg's trying to get me arrested."

"What did you do?"

"I didn't do anything." She was annoyed. "Peg said I was pursuing her car with my car. Can you imagine that?"

"Were you?" Julie looked unconvinced.

"How can you even ask me that?" She thought Julie was on her side. Your lover was supposed to support you no matter what.

"Don't get so excited."

She slammed her hand on the table. "You'd get excited too if you were me. It sounds like you believe Peg."

"Hey," Kathy said, coming through the swinging doors. "Cut the noise out here. You know better than that, Sylvia."

"All right, I'll go." She was crying now, feeling abandoned by everyone. Why was she always at fault?

"Wait, Sylvia. I didn't mean anything. I wouldn't blame you if you did try to run her down." Julie came around the table and took her by the arms.

"Okay. All right, darling," she said quickly, glad to accept her apology. She turned to Kathy. "Sorry. I'll keep my voice down." She put a finger to her lips as a promise.

180

XIV

A meeting had been scheduled for February tenth with Sylvia and her new attorney, George Hardell. Sylvia had allowed an appraisal by someone Peg had chosen. The appraiser told Peg that Sylvia claimed the water heater needed replacing and the new roof leaked around the skylights during heavy rain, that the roofers hadn't been able to fix it. Sylvia also maintained that the new furnace they'd had installed didn't put out enough heat. He said he'd found minor staining around the skylights, but he hadn't been able to get up on the roof to check further. And the water heater was older. Did Peg know how old? But the furnace should be more than adequate, he thought.

Now she understood why the last appraisal had been low. Sylvia had sabotaged it by pointing out defects that weren't there. The roof hadn't leaked while she lived under it, nor had the water heater malfunctioned, and she'd never been cold because of the furnace. She was angry to the point of tears.

"What do I do? Call in a plumber, a roofer, and a furnace man? In all probability, she won't let them near the place, and they'll cost me more money." She spoke to Lauren after talking to the appraiser.

"Why don't you take the loss and get on with things?" Lauren said, sketching her with rapid strokes.

"I don't look my best right now. Why are you drawing me?"

"I want to catch you in all your moods."

"I'm tired of being angry."

"Then get this house business over with. The sooner she's out of your life the better off you'll be."

"Easy for you to say. You aren't losing anything."

"Look at it this way. The more you piss away trying to outsmart her the less you have for us. But it's you I want, not money."

Peg stared at Lauren for a long moment, thinking about her part in all this. Moving in on a friend's relationship wasn't exactly kosher, even if that relationship stank. "What do you tell people about us? If someone asks how we met, what do you say?"

Lauren stopped sketching and stared back. "I'm not proud of what we did, you know that."

"How long have we been together? Since we

started fucking? Since we got caught? Since I left Sylvia?" She felt a surge of anger. Lauren was as much to blame as she was, yet she wasn't getting ripped off.

"Good question. How do you answer it?" Lauren looked thoughtful.

"When we move in together, it'll be day one. I'd rather not talk about the rest of it."

Placing her sketch pad on the floor, Lauren patted her lap. "Come here, sweetie."

Peg turned away. "I'm going to the library."

"Let's not destroy our relationship, Peg. That would please Sylvia." Lauren was on her feet. "I'll go with you."

"You don't have to." She felt very tired. What had Lauren to lose in all this? "Are you happy, Lauren?" She pulled on her jacket and picked up the books she had to return.

"When you are, Peg. Are you blaming me for everything?" The blue eyes searched hers.

"No. We were both at fault, but you had less to lose."

"I didn't seduce you, Peg."

"I know."

It made Sylvia furious whenever she thought of having to pay Peg anything for her equity in the house. She'd done her best to ensure that the appraisals were low, but she'd still have to buy Peg's share and pay closing costs and renegotiate at the going rate. All because Peg wanted out. It wasn't fair.

And now Julie wanted to move in. She could drag out a settlement interminably, inconveniencing Peg. But it would impact on her too. She wouldn't be able to make improvements because if she did upgrade the house, it might cost her more when she and Peg eventually settled — unless they could sort that out.

Her new attorney had encouraged her to agree on a monetary value for the house when they met with Peg and Hannah Alexander. He had suggested that she and Peg use the difference between the two appraisals as a fair asking price. He'd also urged her to figure the joint possessions into that amount — things like the stove and refrigerator. She'd have to wait until she saw Peg's appraisal before agreeing to anything. If it was close to hers, she might do it.

A thought crawled into her mind every time she thought of dishing out money for the house. If she or Peg died while they owned the house together, the survivor would become sole owner because of the way the mortgage read.

They were meeting at Hardell's office this time. She parked in the lot behind the building that housed Hardell, Hardell, Clark & Frobisher along with four other floors of professionals. Hunching into her collar, she hurried inside and took the elevator to the third floor. Hanging up her coat, she made herself known to the receptionist, who notified George Hardell.

When Peg and Hannah Alexander arrived, Sylvia was waiting with Hardell in the conference room. Warm sunshine poured through the window. Outside, its heat had been negligible in the windy day. The greetings were brief and to the point. The two sides sat across the table from each other.

"Do you have your appraisal with you?" Hardell asked. A small, dapper man, he was all business.

Hannah passed across the appraisal that placed the worth of the house at one hundred nineteen thousand, nine hundred dollars, and Sylvia reached for it.

Peg asked in a cold, dispassionate voice, "Why did you lie to the appraiser, Sylvia?"

"Let me handle this, Peg," Hannah said, putting a hand on her arm. "The person who appraised the house for Ms. Doyle said Ms. Everett told him that the skylights leaked during heavy rains, that the water heater was insufficient, and that the new furnace wasn't putting out enough Btu's. Is that correct, Ms. Everett?"

Stunned by the value placed on the house by Peg's appraiser, Sylvia said, "That's right. All those things are true. So how did he come up with this price?"

Hardell attempted to resume control of the meeting. "Can we compromise here? Maybe go with one hundred fourteen thousand, nine hundred."

"There are also the costs of the stove and refrigerator and some of the furnishings that Ms. Doyle left behind," Hannah countered.

"Have you got values on those?" he asked.

"Wait a minute," Sylvia said sharply, "The stove and refrigerator were included in the earlier appraisal, and she's got most of the joint possessions."

Hardell looked at her. "You agree to one hundred fourteen thousand, nine hundred then?"

She frowned. The house would sell for more than that, she knew, but she had no intention of listing it, and she was the one who would have to pay closing costs when the mortgage was renegotiated.

When they'd bought it, they had each made a ten-thousand-dollar down payment and then spent more than five thousand apiece in improvements. They had managed to whittle the mortgage down to less than seventy thousand. Quickly figuring, Sylvia thought Peg would get close to twenty-three thousand dollars out of the deal. A rip-off, considering what the house might sell for on the open market.

"I agree to it," Peg said.

Sylvia snapped, "You still haven't told me where this appraiser got his figures."

"Let's put it on the market, Sylvia. Let it bring an honest price." Peg gave her a baleful look. "Or better yet, I'll buy the house."

"Oh, no," she said, alarmed. She hadn't expected Peg to make an offer. The house was hers. She had stayed with it and paid the mortgage and the other bills. "You just agreed to let it go for one hundred fourteen nine." She turned to Hardell. "What does she get out of that?"

"Half of the difference between the appraisal and the balance of the mortgage."

"That's what I thought." She took a deep breath. "Okay. I'll buy it."

Sylvia guessed that Peg thought she'd gotten around her. No way. She refused to lock into the present mortgage rates. They were too damn high. She told her attorney before leaving his office that she'd wait until they came down a point and a half.

"All I said was that I'd pay one hundred fourteen, nine for the house. I didn't say when."

"That's true, but the assumption was that you'd set a closing date as soon as possible."

"I will, when it's advantageous."

"You should have been an attorney, Sylvia. Then we would have earned our reputation," Hardell said.

Now what did he mean by that? she wondered as she got into her car. Did he think she would be so stupid as to refinance at nearly nine percent when it was possible that she might get the loan at seven and a half or less if she was patient?

Puttering around the house later that afternoon before leaving for the café, she came across an old bottle of sleeping pills that belonged to Peg. If this were that Angela Lansbury program, she'd inject the capsules with rat poison and mail them to Peg. As it was, she could only hope that Peg would obligingly drop dead before closing. However, since she was the one who was going to be fifty next year, it was more likely she'd bite the dust.

Would she have the nerve to off Peg if the opportunity presented itself? She sat down and looked at the bottle of pills. When she'd followed Peg's car onto 441, she'd fought back the urge to ram her Tempo with the Volvo.

Ach, she couldn't do such a thing. Batting away the thought, she tried to conjure up Peg. She'd seen her only that afternoon, and yet she couldn't get a clear picture of her. Did she care about her at all anymore? She was contemplating the question when the phone rang, causing her to jump and bark a hello.

"Sylvia, it's Deirdre. Would you like a ride to the café with me and Phyllis?"

"Okay, sure. What time, though?"

"You all right, Sylvia?"

"Yes. I was deep in thought, is all. Around five?"

"More like five-thirty. Tell me everything tonight. I don't have time to talk now."

When Deirdre rang the doorbell at five forty-five, Sylvia glared at her. "Sorry, we're late. Phyllis and I are going to have to move in together in order to synchronize our time." Deirdre paused. "You're mad, aren't you?"

"Let's just go." She'd been waiting with her jacket on since shortly after five.

The Pontiac's engine hummed, its small interior offering a warm haven. Phyllis turned as she climbed into the backseat behind Deirdre. "Pretty night, isn't it? All those stars flung like jacks across the sky, and a new moon getting ready to set."

"No wonder it's freezing out. Clear nights are colder." That should silence Phyllis. She hadn't had much use for her since she'd said she thought Lauren was nice. "It'd be a pretty night in Mexico." She and Peg had usually gone there for a winter vacation in late February or early March.

"We made reservations to fly to Cancun for a week next month," Deirdre said, pausing at the end of the driveway to peer past the mounds of snow. "Are you going anywhere this winter?"

Sylvia was envious. "Julie doesn't have time or money. It's too late now anyway."

"With the Mexican economy the way it is and the dollar so strong against the peso, we decided we couldn't pass up a vacation there," Phyllis pointed out.

"Lucky you." She stared at the homes they were

passing, whose lights spilled outside onto shrubs and snow. How warm and friendly they looked, beacons in the bitter night. Of course, their beckoning warmth was a deceitful illusion, like most things. The inhabitants would no more welcome her knock on their door than she would theirs.

"I was wondering if you would take care of Ernestine while I'm gone?" Deirdre asked, eyeing her in the rearview mirror.

Deirdre's cat was a gray furball, who concealed herself whenever anyone visited. She'd taken care of her in the past. It meant going over every few days to check the furtive cat's water and food dishes and its litter box. She might need a favor from Deirdre sometime, so she said, "Sure. When are you leaving?"

"March tenth."

In the café kitchen a kettle of soup steamed on the stove. It smelled wonderful.

Julie looked up from the preparation table. "You're late, Sylvia."

"I rode with Deirdre and Phyllis. Blame them. Besides, I don't work here." She kissed Julie's cheek, which smelled of onions. "You taste delicious."

Julie laughed. "Get out of here. I smell like food."

"And I'm hungry." She buried her cold nose in Julie's hot neck, raising giggles.

Jimmy squinted through the smoke-filled atmosphere at Peg. "What are you going to do with twenty-three thou, honey? Buy a house?"

"That's my plan. I have to talk to Lauren, though." The two of them were waiting at one of the gay bars for Lauren and Cal to show up before ordering the Friday night fish dinner.

"Are you going to draw up a prenuptial agreement?"

"Lauren wouldn't cheat me." He'd known Lauren longer than she had.

"We never think that, do we? Besides I remember you saying you wouldn't buy another house with anyone without a partnership agreement." He sipped his drink, gazing at her over his glass.

"Don't do this, Jimmy. You're trying to make me doubt her." She detected amusement in the glitter of his eyes.

"If I were you, I'd doubt everyone."

"You told me once that you'd trust Lauren with your life," she persisted, needing him to corroborate her belief in Lauren.

His gaze shifted to the wall over her shoulder, as if staring at a memory. "She's a faithful friend, as true as a dog. She stuck by me in my year of need when my lover was dying, and I love her dearly for it." Meeting her eyes, he added, "But lovers are only friends as long as they remain devoted to each other. If that changes, they become the most devious and untrustworthy people. Right? Think of yourself."

"What is this?" But it was true. Her guilt made her defensive. "You said Sylvia deserved everything she got."

"I did and she does. What I'm saying is that people are unpredictable, that it's better to take a few precautions."

The back door opened, admitting Lauren and Cal along with a whiff of cold air that set the stagnant smoke into momentary motion. "They're here," she said as Jimmy turned to follow her gaze.

He stood up. "Right this way," he said, motioning toward their table.

Sitting next to her, Lauren searched her eyes. "How did it go this afternoon?"

"She agreed to settle for one fourteen nine. The house is worth more, but I took your advice and let it go."

"How do you feel about it?" Lauren asked, looking worried.

She knew the varying shades of Lauren's eyes, the cues written in her expressive face, as well as she'd known the signs of Sylvia's incipient anger. "I'll feel better when it's done. She could still back out."

Speaking slowly, Lauren searched her face. "I don't want to think, nor do I want you to think, that you made this decision because I said you should let go."

"You did tell me to get on with it." She felt inexplicably contrary.

"It's been eating at you, Peg. You needed to end it."

"I offered to buy the house. She didn't expect it. That's what pushed her into agreement."

"Did you want it?" Lauren looked surprised.

"At that moment I did. It's too pricey for me, but it's a lovely house. Would you have lived in it with me?" The question was a challenge.

"Probably."

Jimmy rapped on the table. "Ladies, it's rude to exclude us from the conversation."

"I was telling her about the meeting this afternoon."

Cal asked, "Did you settle?"

She nodded.

"I think you should buy the first round, honey, now that you've got a few thousand to spare." Jimmy winked at her.

A few thousand minus attorney fees, appraisal, cost of moving, lost possessions, lost equity, the expenses inherent in buying another house. But, as usual, she found it impossible to be annoyed for long with him.

XV

Peg began perusing real estate ads and dragging Lauren to open houses after the February meeting. She asked a real estate agent to send her listings. Not sure what kind of home Lauren would be interested in buying, she was afraid to ask for fear Lauren would say she didn't want a house. But Lauren's obvious lack of interest was something she couldn't ignore.

On Saturday, a month and a day from the February tenth meeting, she told Lauren that she wanted to delay her moving until they bought a house together. Why make the effort twice?

A swatch of sunlight spread inward from the kitchen window, catching Lauren in its path. She looked hot and annoyed, her face red. "Sylvia hasn't renegotiated the mortgage. You can't buy until she does, and who knows when that'll be. And I'm not sure I want to live in a house. I like my flat. There's no upkeep, no mowing, no shoveling."

It was a reminder that she'd heard nothing about a closing date. "I'd better call Hannah and find out what's going on," she said worriedly.

"If you don't want to move in with me, don't." Lauren was chopping cabbage on the butcher block, her curls an angelic blonde in the sun's rays.

"Look, I sleep here nearly every night. We spend weekends here. I may as well be moved in." She glanced outside longingly and picked up a green pepper to dice. As 'soon as they finished the slaw, they would go for a walk.

Lauren paused and looked at her out of angry blue eyes. "Living together is what makes a relationship a commitment."

"You just told me you don't want to buy a house together," she said, hurt and dismayed. "So, where do we go from here?"

"We can't go anywhere until you financially kiss good-bye to Sylvia."

They should have discussed a financial future, which made her realize they had never talked about a life together as if assuming there would be none.

They had not shared their expectations, their hopes. It was like starting from scratch. She opened a window. The day was exceptionally warm. "What do you want from me, Lauren?"

"You used to ask me that when we were having an affair." Lauren attacked the cabbage, chopping it and dumping the pieces into a bowl.

"That was in a different context. We're trying to put together a relationship now, and we don't know what we need from each other or even where or how we want to live. We never talked about that stuff." Finishing with the pepper, Peg peeled an onion.

Lauren said, "I know. I guess I thought it would all work out once Sylvia was out of the picture, that we would live happily ever after. Stupid of me." She smiled, her sunny disposition surfacing. "I'll make a deal. If we do find a house we both like, we'll buy it. Until then, I want you to move in with me. It's March already."

Not quite outmaneuvered, Peg said, "I'll tell you what. We'll move all my clothes and personal things and keep the heavy stuff stored as long as we're looking at houses."

"Good thinking," Lauren agreed. "I forgot it's three flights of stairs. Jimmy would kill us if we made him help haul everything up here, only to move it again."

"I'll see if he wants me to put my things in storage."

When she asked him, they were loading her clothes into his Bronco the next day to take them to

Lauren's. He said, "Are you crazy, woman? I don't want to move everything three times. Twice is bad enough."

"I'll miss living with you, Jimmy. Are you going to ask Cal to move in?"

Isolated clumps of snow hid from the sun on the north sides of ditches and buildings and in groves of trees. The temperature had soared from zero at the beginning of the month to the sixties this second weekend. Her spirits had risen with the thermometer. The end of winter excited her almost as much as cutting her ties with Sylvia.

"I have asked him."

"I should get my things out then, so he has room for his," she said quickly, transferring the clothes from her arms to the Ford.

"He didn't say yes. Maybe later was his answer." He squinted, standing bareheaded and jacketless in the record warm afternoon. "Another spring. Makes it all worthwhile, doesn't it?"

"Yes." She leaned against her car, parked next to his. How nice it was to stand around with only a T-shirt between her and the weather. "I'm going to load my car up now. You can go ahead if you want. I know you're in a hurry."

"It's just that I have to meet Cal after four."

"I understand. I'll lock up." She turned to go back in the house. Lauren had stayed at the flat, making room in her closets and drawers.

Carrying downstairs a box of books that she wanted with her, she shunted it in her trunk among her toiletries and suitcases. There were more clothes in the backseat along with her CD collection, bedding, the painting her parents had given her. Jimmy had her radio/tape deck/CD player with speakers, her small color TV, video player, and a couple of lamps. The rest of her things she left behind, knowing she could retrieve them anytime.

Locking the house, she climbed behind the wheel and started the car. When she turned on to 441, she glanced at the fuel gauge and was shocked to see that it registered empty. The bypass carried almost no cars as it had the afternoon she'd encountered Sylvia on it. If she ran out of gas, she'd have to walk. She decided to get off at Oneida Street and fill up at the Citgo station where she sometimes washed her car.

Between KK and Oneida the Tempo jerked a couple times, regained speed, then jerked once more and started slowing down within a hundred feet of the exit ramp. "Come on, come on," she urged, knowing it was no use wishing. She pulled onto the berm as the engine died and the steering wheel locked in place. Sitting inside the vehicle for a few moments, she considered her options. A passing pickup rocked the car. She decided to walk to Oneida and cross over to the Piggly Wiggly, where she could call Lauren. Taking some money, she locked her purse in the car under the clothes.

The wind pierced her T-shirt, making her wish she had worn a sweatshirt. Hearing tires on the pavement behind her, she hugged the edge of the berm, nearly treading on the grass. When her peripheral vision spotted the car bearing down on her, she half turned. Its fender grazed her arm, and she jumped toward the embankment, rolling to a stop in the grass at the bottom. The car continued, turning right on to Oneida without stopping. She was left with only fleeting impressions. A large vehicle with dark paint, like Sylvia's Volvo. But she could never identify it. She hadn't seen the make or the license plate, much less the driver.

Nearby lay a rotting carcass. Its snakelike tail told her it was a possum. Road kill. Looking around from a prone position, she saw no witnesses. Just her luck. Her heart jumped around in her chest like a wild thing. Shakily, she stood and attempted to brush herself off. Her left arm wouldn't function. She took hold of it with her right hand, and held it against her body. Sure that it was broken, she wondered why there wasn't more pain. Unbalanced, she made unsteady progress off the exit ramp.

From the Piggly Wiggly, where a nice woman had taken her in her car, she called Lauren's flat. Leaning her head against the wall between the outer and inner doors, she waited for Lauren to answer.

Horrified at what she had done yet more scared of being caught than she was repentant, Sylvia drove carefully through the streets. She'd taken 441 to meet Julie at a craft show on the northeast side of town. Afterward, Julie had left for the café and she'd taken the same route as earlier toward home. When she'd seen Peg walking away from her car, Sylvia'd been thinking about having to remortgage the house. A rage had swept over her and she'd found herself trying to run her down.

Surprised to be in her own driveway, she hurried into the house. In the bathroom mirror, she stared at a face without color out of eyes huge and black. "I

198

hit her; I know I did," she said to her reflection and then clamped a hand over her mouth.

Thumping down on the toilet lid, she clutched the area where her heart threatened to pound out of her chest. She felt light-headed. Gradually, the beating slowed and her breathing normalized. "I wonder if she's okay." Had anyone seen? She didn't think so.

She might have to account for her time. No one knew she'd taken 441. She'd say she took AP to KK to the craft show and came back the same way. But there was good reason for her to want rid of Peg. Everyone knew she resented having to pay her. Concluding that she was too nervous to commit crimes, she thought she better set a closing date tomorrow morning.

Glad that Julie wasn't coming over, she turned on the television and stared at it. Maybe what happened would be on the news. Scanning channels, she was unable to watch anything for long. Then she realized that she needed to go to Deirdre's and look in on Ernestine. She should do it before dark.

Driving to Deirdre's apartment meant going near Lauren's flat. She saw no familiar cars in the space next to the building. Parking out front at Deirdre's, she let herself into the stuffy apartment. Sighting the elusive cat taking refuge behind the davenport, she gave a harsh laugh. "I'd hide too. Killer's here."

Making a face, she cleaned the turds out of the litter box, changed the water, and added fresh food to the cat's dish. She jumped when the animal brushed against her leg. "Lonesome, huh?" she said, bending down to pat the feline. But it hightailed down the hall and out of sight.

When she drove past again, two unfamiliar cars

were parked next to Lauren's building. She continued home, hoping that Peg was all right, that she hadn't killed her. Tears streamed down her face at the thought of never seeing Peg again.

In one of the hospital emergency rooms, Peg watched the splint being fastened to her arm, which throbbed in its casing. A plaster cast would take its place when the swelling was down. Lauren sat in the lone chair while Peg lay on the narrow examining table with the resident doctor and nurse working over her.

"Feeling better?" the doctor asked.

She'd been woozy earlier in the X-ray room. "I'm okay." But this felt like a dream. Not even Sylvia would try to kill her. She wondered if Jimmy and Cal had filled her car and gotten it off the bypass before it was towed away.

"You're lucky. You said you were hit by a car, that it was a hit-and-run? Have you called the police?"

"We did," Lauren said, filling in the silence while Peg tried to remember.

"No witnesses, though?" the doctor persisted.

"I didn't see any." Wanting to laugh, she pictured herself lying in last year's grass next to the possum carcass, raising her head like a turtle to scout for safety and spotting the dead animal.

Two uniformed officers showed up while she lay on the table and questioned her for details. She answered as best she could, wanting to get the inquiry over so that she could go home to bed. She knew they'd never arrest anyone. There wasn't enough evidence.

"Why didn't you tell them you thought it was Sylvia?" Lauren asked, helping her into the pickup, carefully protecting her arm.

"I didn't see the car well enough to identify it, Lauren. I told you that." She'd taken a pain pill, and now she wanted to lie down in the worst way. Vomit kept climbing up her throat.

"They could talk to her. She needs a good scare." Lauren turned the key, and the truck's engine rattled to life. "If you die while your name is still on the mortgage, that house becomes hers, doesn't it?"

It was true, but she didn't want to talk about it. Resting her head against the back of the seat, she let Lauren fasten her into the seat belt. "Take me home, sweetie. I don't feel so good."

Her Tempo was parked in the building's small lot, as was Jimmy's Bronco. When she realized that she'd have to climb all those steps, she nearly asked to go to Jimmy's house. But then Jimmy clambered down the stairs and helped Lauren haul her up to the flat.

Lauren took her clothes off and put her to bed. Peg was no help. She kept drifting into sleep. Later, when the windows were dark, she awakened and heard voices in the other room. She thought she recognized one of the policemen talking. But she couldn't stay awake to identify it.

Monday morning Sylvia called the bank that held the mortgage. She told them that Peg would be signing a quitclaim deed and that she'd be taking out another mortgage in her name alone. Could they draw up the papers and give her a date?

She had watched the local news that morning. There had been a hit-and-run yesterday on 441, in which the victim suffered a broken arm. The police were investigating. Tonight she was sure they would be knocking on her door. Well, renegotiating the mortgage would free her of motive.

One of the phone lines lit up, and Judy buzzed her. Her heart hammered guiltily. She had to get hold of this fear before it gave her away. "Sylvia Everett speaking."

The officer identified himself. "Ms. Everett, would you come down to the police station by the court-house this morning and answer some questions?"

"About what?" Taking a deep breath, she told herself to sound annoyed, not nervous. She had to pretend she knew nothing. "I'm busy."

"We can send someone to get you, but I thought you'd rather come in yourself."

"What do you want?"

"We'll tell you when you get here."

By the time she parked in front of the station, she had found her anger and wrapped it around herself. Peg deserved a scare. She'd deny she'd been on 441. No one could prove it. She stalked into headquarters with her head high.

"Take a seat, Ms. Everett. Someone will be with you soon," a uniformed woman told her.

"I hope so. My time is costly." Pleased to hear the snap back in her tone, she drew herself up and sat in a hard chair nearby. She looked around for magazines, but there was nothing to read.

The man striding toward her looked familiar. "Will you come with me please, Ms. Everett?"

She followed him to a corner desk and sat in the chair next to it. Watching him fiddle through some papers, she fought back apprehension. It would be nice to have more privacy, she thought, looking around. When she felt she couldn't wait another minute for him to break the silence, he raised his head and she recognized him. He'd been at the house the day Peg moved — the older policeman, the one who'd been so impatient. Her heart thumped so loud she thought he would hear it.

"I'm Officer Tom Drexler. Do you remember me?"

"Yes. Why did you ask me to come here?" Pig, she thought. He wore his hair in a crew cut, had small eyes and a pug nose. He looked the part.

"There was a hit-and-run on 441 yesterday. Perhaps you saw it on the news." He waited, apparently for a reaction, but she gave him none. "Where were you yesterday afternoon between three and four?"

"At a craft show in Darboy with my friend, Julie Peterson."

"Did you drive with her?" His small eyes studied her intently.

"No." She would offer no information. He'd have to ask for it.

"You drove alone?" She nodded. "What route did you take there and back?"

"AP to Double K. Look, I saw no hit-and-run. I can tell you that much. Why are you asking me?"

"The victim was Peg Doyle." She swore his eyes narrowed.

Trying to sound surprised, she said, "Peg? Is she all right?"

"She was lucky. Her arm was broken. Highway 441 would have been the logical route for you to take to KK. Why did you drive on AP?"

"I like looking at the new houses. It's more interesting."

He stood up abruptly. "Thanks for coming in, Ms. Everett. We'll call you if we need you."

Back in the Volvo, she went over the questioning in her head. Her armpits were wet. She drove back to the office slowly, hardly noticing the traffic. Damn. Why had she panicked and arranged for closing?

Alone in the flat the next day, Peg slept off and on. She didn't understand why she could hardly stay awake. Lauren, who had kissed her good-bye around eight in the morning, called at ten.

"How are you feeling, darling?"

"Sleepy. How are you?"

"Worried. Keep the door locked. I'll come home at lunchtime."

"Nothing's going to happen to me, Lauren."

Jimmy called shortly after Lauren hung up. "How are you, honey?"

"I'm so tired."

"You're probably still in shock," he said. "It's not every day somebody tries to kill you."

"You're as bad as Lauren. No one tried to kill me. It was probably someone who wasn't paying attention." She'd nearly run off the road many times while searching for a tape or something in her purse.

"Why didn't they stop then?"

"Maybe the person was afraid of getting a ticket, or maybe they never saw me."

"Have it your way, Peggy. I gotta go. I'll stop by after work."

At noon she took a few spoonfuls of the tomato soup Lauren warmed for her, then went back to sleep as Lauren watched. When she woke up next, she was alone. Padding to the bathroom, she grabbed her book from the other room and took it back to bed with her.

Jimmy brought Chinese carryout with him that evening. He set the little white boxes on the table. She sat at the table, while Lauren brought out plates and forks. Lauren argued against her going back to work tomorrow, but she held her own.

"I'm all slept out. If I get too tired, I'll come home." Her worry centered around working her computer with only one hand. The search and peck method was slow. She'd get way behind.

"Will you look both ways before you cross the street, honey?" Jimmy implored.

"I always do." She wouldn't admit it, but they had convinced her that she was in danger. In one day she'd gone from denial that Sylvia would ever try to do her in to believing that Sylvia had attempted to run her down. God knows, it wasn't so hard to imagine Sylvia becoming enraged enough at the sight of her to lose control.

XVI
April 26, 1995

Closing was scheduled the afternoon of Peg's thirty-eighth birthday. She had left the signed quitclaim deed in the hands of Hannah Alexander, who would represent her for the short time it took to close. She resented spending hard-earned money to pay an attorney for something she herself could do, but she could not bring herself to meet with Sylvia. Besides, the cast was scheduled for removal that day.

Leaving work at four in the afternoon, she drove to the clinic on Midway Road. She was reading in the waiting room, when Kathy Gordon sat next to her.

"You're looking good," Kathy said.

"So are you. Why are you here?" she asked.

"Waiting for Jeanne. She has heel spurs." Kathy tapped the cast. "How's it going?"

"It's coming off today. I appreciated the calls and the cards."

"We were worried about you. You never identified the car?"

"Nope. It happened too fast. All I know is it was big and dark." She bit her tongue to keep from saying the obvious.

Kathy said it for her. "Like Sylvia's."

A nurse called her name and she stood up. "Give my best to Jeanne."

"You and Lauren come by the café. We'll buy you dinner."

"Thanks. One of these days we will."

When she left the doctor's office, Kathy was gone from the waiting room. She and Lauren had planned a picnic at High Cliff that afternoon for a birthday celebration. Her arm looked pitiful, all peeling and mottled. It ached without the cast and had been bent too long for her to immediately straighten it.

"Jimmy's going to meet us at the park. I told him we'd be down below, near the marina." Lauren greeted her at the door. "Wonderful out, isn't it? How's the arm?"

She smiled at Lauren's enthusiastic welcome. "It aches, and I can't bend it."

"Happy birthday, sweetheart." Lauren bent to hug and kiss her.

She pressed her arm protectively against her body. "Do you remember what happened a year ago today?"

"The day we got caught. How could I forget? Nightmares sometimes do come true." Lauren released her carefully. "Are you ready to go?"

"Today was closing," she said, recalling that six years ago today she and Sylvia had signed the mortgage together.

"I know." Lauren flashed her a smile as she loaded the picnic basket in the bed of her truck. "It's almost all over."

She pictured the car looming on her left side and thought she'd be looking behind her for Sylvia the rest of her life. Glancing out the window, she watched the greening landscape pass by.

Jimmy's Bronco was parked near the shelter closest to the marina. He was flying a kite, which looked very much like a swooping, diving orange air mattress. As they walked toward him, he hollered, "It's the next best thing to flying." Then he tied it to a picnic table and helped them carry the food.

A brisk wind blew off the open water, cooling the sun-heated air. The lake dazzled in the bright day, its waves glinting with reflected light. Peg sniffed the water, redolent with animal and plant life cast on the shore. A moment of pure exhilaration shot through her. Winter was over and life was good.

Uncorking the wine he had brought for the occasion, Jimmy toasted her birthday, the closing, the cast coming off.

Suddenly shy, she lifted her plastic cup. "Thanks, both of you, for getting me through the past year."

* * * * *

"Where's Peg?" Sylvia asked Hannah Alexander. "Isn't she coming?"

"No. I'm taking care of it for her."

"Can she do that?" she asked the closing agent, a woman from the title company.

"No need for her to be here as long as the necessary papers are signed."

"I won't close without her," she said angrily. "Call her and make her come." She wanted to see her.

The title company woman, whose name Sylvia had already forgotten, said, "We can call off the closing, but you'll forfeit your up-front money."

Fuck, she thought. She couldn't afford to lose the origination fee she'd already paid, and she'd been lucky to get an interest rate equal to the one on the old mortgage. The papers were drawn up. She'd have to let it go. "Where do I sign?" she muttered.

"Do you have the cashier's check made out to Ms. Doyle?" the woman asked.

Sylvia handed the check to Hannah Alexander. The closing agent took the quitclaim deed to register with the mortgage. It was done. Pushing back her chair, she went out into the afternoon. She felt let down.

As she climbed in her new Volvo, which looked like a twin of her old one, she remembered it was Peg's birthday. A year ago she'd caught Lauren and Peg in an embrace. Since then, her life had spiraled out of control. Now she could begin anew. The house was hers. But the sense of anticlimax clung to her.

Her anger toward Peg had diminished, culminating with the hit-and-run. She told herself that her attempt to run down Peg had been a freak occurrence, that it would never happen again. When she thought of it, she felt liquid fear course through her. She'd risked her reputation, her good name. Some people thought she was responsible, she knew — the police and Kathy Gordon for sure. Their suspicions irritated her.

Tonight, after dinner, Julie was moving in with her. Outside of clothes and toiletries, lots of them, Julie had hardly anything to move. Jeanne was helping, but Kathy had said she'd hold down the café, which suited Sylvia just fine. She didn't want anyone around who thought she was capable of murder.

Glancing at herself in the rearview mirror, she admired her new hairstyle. Her do, as Julie referred to it, was short and curly with feathered hair softening her face. Every month Julie tried some new vogue on her. Julie did her makeup, her nails. She felt like a fashion plate.

Driving to the café, she found Julie in the kitchen. "Peg didn't show up for the closing."

"That's good," Julie said absently. "I've been thinking, Sylvia."

"Yes, what have you been thinking, sweetheart?" she encouraged, putting on an apron and washing her hands.

"Would you mind if I did a few cuts and perms at the house?"

Intensely adverse to the idea of her home being invaded by strangers, Sylvia thought quickly and said, "It's not zoned for business."

"I wouldn't put out a sign or anything."

"Can't you get a chair in a shop?" She shredded lettuce with practiced speed and annoyance.

"I could, but then I'd have to pay the shop owner. This way I'd get on my feet faster."

Frowning into Julie's brown eyes, she said, "I don't like the idea." Whose house was it anyway? She sensed her life getting out of hand again.

Julie smiled. "All right, I'll look for a chair somewhere else."

The sudden capitulation threw her off balance. She didn't trust it.

After Jeanne unloaded her car and left that night, Sylvia helped Julie carry her clothes to the spare bedroom where Peg had once kept hers. She had hauled an old dresser and a chair out of the attic and placed them in the room emptied of Peg's belongings.

At thirty-five years of age, Julie had no furniture, not even a bed. "What do I need with furniture? It's just more stuff to move."

"Did you move a lot?" She was handing Julie hangers to put her clothes on.

"What can you do if someone wants you out, except go?"

"I agree." She considered being kept against her will. She would hate it.

"Do you love me?" Julie asked.

She hesitated. "Yes, do you love me?"

"Why else would I be here?" Julie replied, sticking her head out of the closet and giving her a smacking kiss on the mouth.

On Thursday noon, Peg picked up the check from Hannah Alexander. "I'll be able to pay you now." She had yet to be billed. "Thanks for everything, Hannah. It was a mess, and you got me out of it."

Hannah shook her hand. "You got yourself out of it. I'm glad I was able to help. I never figured Sylvia out."

"Neither did I. I thought I knew her, but I'm not sure Sylvia's a real person."

Pointing her toward the chair in front of her desk, Hannah sat down. "What do you mean, Peg?"

"She's like a chameleon, always changing colors. Sometimes I think she needs someone to define herself. She certainly has to have someone to show her how to behave."

"And yet she runs her own business and, I gather, is successful at it."

"Very. But she gets in people's faces, she offends without meaning to, she is offended when she shouldn't be. Her temper is legendary. Her picture of reality is skewed by her past."

"Did she grow up in an abusive family?"

"She said she did, and she's abusive when angered. If you can't walk away from abuse, you end up using it as a weapon yourself." In the end she had responded to Sylvia's abuse with like behavior. "Well, I have to get back to work."

She stopped at the credit union and deposited the check in her savings account. Tonight she and Lauren were going to meet with the real estate agent at a house near High Cliff. They had seen the for-sale sign last night.

Putting her purse in her desk drawer, she sat behind her computer at work. Each desk was partitioned off, giving the impression of privacy, but she could see Robb's desk from hers. He had taken on some of her work when she was in the cast. She had wrapped her arm with an Ace bandage today to give it some support. It eased the ache.

"Did you get your money?" Robb asked.

"It's already in the bank."

"I'll buy you a drink tonight," he offered.

"Thanks, but I can't. We're going to look at a house. I'll buy you one after work Friday. I owe you big time." She'd decided that Robb was so confident of who and what he was that he never felt diminished by women, or other men. He could extend himself without worry.

Lauren was at the flat when she got there. She changed into jeans and a T-shirt and they left in the Tempo. Male redwing blackbirds chirped and spread their feathers in courtship and territorial displays in the ditches along Highway 10. Robins pulled worms out of the wet ground. A redtail hawk hovered over the right-of-way. They turned on to 114 and took one of the fire lanes toward the lake.

Peg loved the long, warm, spring evenings that she and Lauren spent outside. When the road reached the lake, she turned east along the north side of Lake Winnebago. The lake carried its usual array of watercraft — sailboats and speedboats of all sizes were scattered across its vast expanse with jet skis and waverunners close to shore. They cut white wakes through waves that mirrored the sky. Dressed in a wetsuit, a person sped along the surface on a sailboard.

"If we live out here, I'll buy a boat," Lauren said, her eyes on the lake.

Peg parked in the gravel driveway behind the real estate agent's car and turned off the engine. "Here

we are. Looks a little rundown, don't you think?"
They gazed at the older two-story house with the
open porch and peeling paint. The garage was
separate and in worse condition. Water pooled in the
middle of the yard.

"Nice location," Lauren answered.

The real estate agent met them as they got out of
the car. "Hello Lauren. Good to see you again, Peg."
She had sold to Peg and Sylvia the house that they
had bought. "This is a fixer-upper. You know that?"
She unlocked the front door and they went inside.
"It's been rental property for the past five years."

The living room was large with worn green shag
carpeting and drywall that desperately needed paint.
Tall windows looked out at the houses bordering the
lake across the road and the side lawn to the east. A
Franklin stove perched on bricks in one corner and
was vented through the sidewall. In a kitchen almost
as big as the living room with torn, stained linoleum
for flooring were white painted cabinets and a walk-
in pantry. From the kitchen windows she saw open
fields. Steps led to a landing where you could either
go outside or on down the basement stairs. The
basement was a frightening dark cavern with bare
bulbs hanging from taped wires.

The two bedrooms on the main floor were
wallpapered with yellowed flowers, their floors covered
by threadless brown carpeting; the front bedroom's
windows looked out at the road and to the west; the
rear bedroom's views were of the backyard and the
west lawn. Oddly, the bathroom off the hall and
between the bedrooms had been modernized with a
knock-down shower encircling a tub, a fairly new
sink, ceramic tile floors, and freshly painted white

walls. All the rooms on the first floor were high ceilinged.

Upstairs were two rooms running the length of the house with bare plank floors and low slanting ceilings. From their windows the lake could be seen in its enormity. What struck her most, she realized as she peered at the water from the upstairs bedrooms, were the large windows. Whoever built the house had wanted lots of light. It gave the illusion of being outside. She would never feel closed up in this house.

The realtor said, "There's lake access at the end of the road for all of the people on this side of the fire lane — a small beach and docking area. Want to see it?"

Glancing at Lauren, who had been quiet, she saw her nod. "Sure," she said.

"And the garage," Lauren added.

When they had viewed it all and were driving home, she asked Lauren, "Well, what did you think?"

"I want it."

Shooting an amazed look at Lauren, she said, "But it needs so much work."

"Under that hideous carpeting are wood floors. We can paint the house inside and out and put down new linoleum in the kitchen. I never thought I'd see a house with enough light to suit me."

"You'd buy a place because there are enough windows?" She was playing the devil's advocate. The lake was the draw for her, as she knew it must be for Lauren too. "We don't have to buy right away. We can look around."

"Hey, the price is right. Sixty-nine nine. It comes with lake access and is close to High Cliff. What

215

more could you want?" Lauren's face was suffused
with light. Her eyes glittered.

"It's cheap because it needs so much work. The
garage is rotting."

"So, let it fall down and build another one. The
house's roof and furnace are fairly new," Lauren
reminded her.

And insulation had been added when the furnace
was installed. "What room would you use as a
studio?" she asked, curious.

"One upstairs, where I can see the lake," Lauren
said without hesitation. "There's not as much light,
but it's a southern exposure."

"This isn't a handy location, you know. It's not
close to stores; it's a much longer drive to work," she
pointed out.

Unable to sleep, they talked late into the night. A
month ago Lauren hadn't even wanted to look at
houses, partly because she didn't want any
maintenance. Now she was keen to buy one that
would keep them busy for months with costly
remodeling. They agreed to offer sixty-five thousand,
nine hundred dollars — contingent upon an inspection.

Saturday afternoon they drove Jimmy past the
house. As they craned their necks, she remembered
what Robb had said when they'd had a drink
together after work yesterday. She'd told him they
were making an offer on a house for the handy-
woman.

"Think of it as recycling." He'd cocked an
eyebrow and lifted a shoulder. "That's what you're
doing, restoring instead of buying new."

It had set her to thinking, had made her willing

to accept the seller's counter offer of sixty-seven thousand, nine hundred as they had this morning. Inspection was set up for next week. Monday she would call Hannah Alexander and ask her to draw up a partnership agreement for Lauren and herself to sign prior to buying the house.

Jimmy said, "Looks like my house did when I bought it — a dump. I can see what I'm going to be doing during my spare time."

They drove to the lake access and walked out on the empty dock. The wind lifted their hair and floated it around their heads as they stood, hands on hips, squinting into the sun. Nothing ever stayed the same, Peg thought, shading her eyes and grinning like a fool. She had learned to savor the joy of the moment.

Epilogue
September 1995

By September Sylvia felt as if she'd lost her home. Julie had set up shop in the basement. As word of mouth circulated around the lesbian community, Julie accumulated customers. On Saturdays, Sylvia let them in the side door and they trooped downstairs for cuts and perms. The perms she thought she could smell clear upstairs in the bedroom. By ten o'clock on most Saturdays she'd left for the office to escape the hair clientele, returning home in the afternoon when Julie called her.

Looking through the real estate ads on the second Sunday she made a suggestion that she'd been considering for weeks. "There's a chair for sale at Mary Jane's Style-It-Right Shop. Did you know that?"

"Is there really?" Julie stood yawning in the kitchen doorway.

"I'll help you buy it, if you want." Her heart thumped at the thought of spending hundreds of dollars on a beautician's chair. But she wanted her house back.

"Honestly, Sylvia?" Julie asked, her face dumb with surprise.

"You have to promise not to do any more hair in the house."

Julie threw her arms around Sylvia's neck. "Cross my heart. Except for yours, of course."

She frowned. What if she set Julie up with her own chair and Julie left her? She often felt manipulated. "We'll draw up a deal."

"And what will it say?"

"I'll give you the money in the form of a loan that's forgiven as long as you live with me. If you leave, you'll have to pay it back with interest."

Narrowing her eyes, Julie whined, "You don't trust me."

"I don't trust anyone completely." She'd trusted Peg. What a mistake that had been. She'd driven past Peg and Lauren's house on the fire lane. When she first heard they'd bought a place together, she'd been devastated. But once she'd seen what a poor example of a house it was, she'd scoffed at them instead. "I think it's a generous offer."

"I'll take it."

Peg and Lauren had worked on the outside of the house through the summer months, scraping and painting, caulking windows, and reinforcing the porch. In August they'd moved inside and begun tearing out carpeting.

Peg was pleased to see that Lauren had been right about the hardwood flooring under the carpets. They'd paid someone to sand the floors while they steamed off wallpaper, repaired cracks, and painted walls. The second weekend in September they removed the linoleum from the kitchen floor and scraped it down.

She and Lauren had fought weekly during this time together. Disgruntled, she struggled to remember their last battle two days ago and failed. Lauren had once said that relationships that began as affairs seldom lasted. Lauren also claimed the two of them struggled with intimacy. Peg thought they fought for the upper hand, neither willing to concede it. Tired of spending weekends and evenings working on the house, she almost wished they hadn't bought it.

"My hands hurt," she said. Jimmy had left a half hour ago for a date with Cal. "Can't we quit?"

"Sure. Want to walk down to the dock?"

Starting down the fire lane, tired from hours of sanding, she automatically glanced behind her.

"Looking for Sylvia?" Lauren asked, untangling her curls with her fingers. "I need a haircut."

"Habit." She never felt easy walking on any road. Glancing at Lauren, she said, "I hear Julie is a good beautician."

Lauren snorted. "I'll stay with mine. He's part of the community too."

"I was trying to remember what our last argument was about, and I couldn't." There was always a breeze off the lake. She pointed her nose toward it and let it wash over her.

"I offended you when I suggested we get an earlier start on the work."

How silly, she thought. They had reached the small public access area with its fenced-in grass. Waves rolled past the posts that held up the dock and over the sandy beach. The water smelled strongly of fish and algae and weeds this time of year. They sat on the wooden surface and dangled their feet over the side.

"I'm sorry. But I won't ever tiptoe around anyone again the way I did Sylvia."

"I don't expect you to," Lauren said, turning a blue-eyed squint on her.

"You know what? I'm actually looking forward to winter, to starting a fire in the Franklin stove, to being shut in with you during a storm." She leaned back on her hands, savoring the peace she felt when they got along. Intimacy hadn't been possible with Sylvia. Why run from it with Lauren?

She pictured their bedroom, filled with light and wind, and the two of them lying in naked embrace. "Want to make love?" That, at least, had never lost its consistent and compelling power.

LAUREL by Isabel Miller. 128 pp. By the author of the beloved
Patience and Sarah. ISBN 1-56280-146-5 $10.95

LOVE OR MONEY by Jackie Calhoun. 240 pp. The romance of
real life. ISBN 1-56280-147-3 10.95

SMOKE AND MIRRORS by Pat Welch. 224 pp. 5th Helen Black
Mystery. ISBN 1-56280-143-0 10.95

DANCING IN THE DARK edited by Barbara Grier & Christine
Cassidy. 272 pp. Erotic love stories by Naiad Press authors.
ISBN 1-56280-144-9 14.95

TIME AND TIME AGAIN by Catherine Ennis. 176 pp. Passionate
love affair. ISBN 1-56280-145-7 10.95

PAXTON COURT by Diane Salvatore. 256 pp. Erotic and wickedly
funny contemporary tale about the business of learning to live
together. ISBN 1-56280-114-7 10.95

INNER CIRCLE by Claire McNab. 208 pp. 8th Carol Ashton
Mystery. ISBN 1-56280-135-X 10.95

LESBIAN SEX: AN ORAL HISTORY by Susan Johnson.
240 pp. Need we say more? ISBN 1-56280-142-2 14.95

BABY, IT'S COLD by Jaye Maiman. 256 pp. 5th Robin Miller
Mystery. ISBN 1-56280-141-4 19.95

WILD THINGS by Karin Kallmaker. 240 pp. By the undisputed
mistress of lesbian romance. ISBN 1-56280-139-2 10.95

THE GIRL NEXT DOOR by Mindy Kaplan. 208 pp. Just what
you'd expect. ISBN 1-56280-140-6 10.95

NOW AND THEN by Penny Hayes. 240 pp. Romance on the
westward journey. ISBN 1-56280-121-X 10.95

HEART ON FIRE by Diana Simmonds. 176 pp. The romantic and
erotic rival of *Curious Wine.* ISBN 1-56280-152-X 10.95

DEATH AT LAVENDER BAY by Lauren Wright Douglas. 208 pp.
1st Allison O'Neil Mystery. ISBN 1-56280-085-X 10.95

YES I SAID YES I WILL by Judith McDaniel. 272 pp. Hot
romance by famous author.   ISBN 1-56280-138-4   10.95

FORBIDDEN FIRES by Margaret C. Anderson. Edited by Mathilda
Hills. 176 pp. Famous author's "unpublished" Lesbian romance.
                                         ISBN 1-56280-123-6   21.95

SIDE TRACKS by Teresa Stores. 160 pp. Gender-bending
Lesbians on the road.   ISBN 1-56280-122-8   10.95

HOODED MURDER by Annette Van Dyke. 176 pp. 1st Jessie
Batelle Mystery.   ISBN 1-56280-134-1   10.95

WILDWOOD FLOWERS by Julia Watts. 208 pp. Hilarious and
heart-warming tale of true love.   ISBN 1-56280-127-9   10.95

NEVER SAY NEVER by Linda Hill. 224 pp. Rule #1: Never get involved
with . . .   ISBN 1-56280-126-0   10.95

THE SEARCH by Melanie McAllester. 240 pp. Exciting top cop
Tenny Mendoza case.   ISBN 1-56280-150-3   10.95

THE WISH LIST by Saxon Bennett. 192 pp. Romance through
the years.   ISBN 1-56280-125-2   10.95

FIRST IMPRESSIONS by Kate Calloway. 208 pp. P.I. Cassidy
James' first case.   ISBN 1-56280-133-3   10.95

OUT OF THE NIGHT by Kris Bruyer. 192 pp. Spine-tingling
thriller.   ISBN 1-56280-120-1   10.95

NORTHERN BLUE by Tracey Richardson. 224 pp. Police recruits
Miki & Miranda — passion in the line of fire. ISBN 1-56280-118-X   10.95

LOVE'S HARVEST by Peggy J. Herring. 176 pp. by the author of
Once More With Feeling.   ISBN 1-56280-117-1   10.95

THE COLOR OF WINTER by Lisa Shapiro. 208 pp. Romantic
love beyond your wildest dreams.   ISBN 1-56280-116-3   10.95

FAMILY SECRETS by Laura DeHart Young. 208 pp. Enthralling
romance and suspense.   ISBN 1-56280-119-8   10.95

INLAND PASSAGE by Jane Rule. 288 pp. Tales exploring conven-
tional & unconventional relationships.   ISBN 0-930044-56-8   10.95

DOUBLE BLUFF by Claire McNab. 208 pp. 7th Carol Ashton
Mystery.   ISBN 1-56280-096-5   10.95

BAR GIRLS by Lauran Hoffman. 176 pp. See the movie, read
the book!   ISBN 1-56280-115-5   10.95

THE FIRST TIME EVER edited by Barbara Grier & Christine
Cassidy. 272 pp. Love stories by Naiad Press authors.
                                         ISBN 1-56280-086-8   14.95

MISS PETTIBONE AND MISS McGRAW by Brenda Weathers.
208 pp. A charming ghostly love story.   ISBN 1-56280-151-1   10.95

CHANGES by Jackie Calhoun. 208 pp. Involved romance and
relationships.   ISBN 1-56280-083-3   10.95

FAIR PLAY by Rose Beecham. 256 pp. 3rd Amanda Valentine
Mystery.   ISBN 1-56280-081-7   10.95

PAYBACK by Celia Cohen. 176 pp. A gripping thriller of romance,
revenge and betrayal.   ISBN 1-56280-084-1   10.95

THE BEACH AFFAIR by Barbara Johnson. 224 pp. Sizzling
summer romance/mystery/intrigue.   ISBN 1-56280-090-6   10.95

GETTING THERE by Robbi Sommers. 192 pp. Nobody does it
like Robbi!   ISBN 1-56280-099-X   10.95

FINAL CUT by Lisa Haddock. 208 pp. 2nd Carmen Ramirez
Mystery.   ISBN 1-56280-088-4   10.95

FLASHPOINT by Katherine V. Forrest. 256 pp. A Lesbian
blockbuster!   ISBN 1-56280-079-5   10.95

CLAIRE OF THE MOON by Nicole Conn. Audio Book —Read
by Marianne Hyatt.   ISBN 1-56280-113-9   16.95

FOR LOVE AND FOR LIFE: INTIMATE PORTRAITS OF
LESBIAN COUPLES by Susan Johnson. 224 pp.
                                             ISBN 1-56280-091-4   14.95

DEVOTION by Mindy Kaplan. 192 pp. See the movie — read
the book!   ISBN 1-56280-093-0   10.95

SOMEONE TO WATCH by Jaye Maiman. 272 pp. 4th Robin
Miller Mystery.   ISBN 1-56280-095-7   10.95

GREENER THAN GRASS by Jennifer Fulton. 208 pp. A young
woman — a stranger in her bed.   ISBN 1-56280-092-2   10.95

TRAVELS WITH DIANA HUNTER by Regine Sands. Erotic
lesbian romp. Audio Book (2 cassettes)   ISBN 1-56280-107-4   16.95

CABIN FEVER by Carol Schmidt. 256 pp. Sizzling suspense
and passion.   ISBN 1-56280-089-1   10.95

THERE WILL BE NO GOODBYES by Laura DeHart Young. 192
pp. Romantic love, strength, and friendship. ISBN 1-56280-103-1   10.95

FAULTLINE by Sheila Ortiz Taylor. 144 pp. Joyous comic
lesbian novel.   ISBN 1-56280-108-2   9.95

OPEN HOUSE by Pat Welch. 176 pp. 4th Helen Black Mystery.
                                             ISBN 1-56280-102-3   10.95

ONCE MORE WITH FEELING by Peggy J. Herring. 240 pp.
Lighthearted, loving romantic adventure.   ISBN 1-56280-089-2   10.95

FOREVER by Evelyn Kennedy. 224 pp. Passionate romance — love
overcoming all obstacles.   ISBN 1-56280-094-9   10.95

WHISPERS by Kris Bruyer. 176 pp. Romantic ghost story
                                             ISBN 1-56280-082-5   10.95

NIGHT SONGS by Penny Mickelbury. 224 pp. 2nd Gianna Maglione
Mystery.   ISBN 1-56280-097-3   10.95

GETTING TO THE POINT by Teresa Stores. 256 pp. Classic
southern Lesbian novel.   ISBN 1-56280-100-7   10.95

PAINTED MOON by Karin Kallmaker. 224 pp. Delicious
Kallmaker romance.   ISBN 1-56280-075-2   10.95

THE MYSTERIOUS NAIAD edited by Katherine V. Forrest &
Barbara Grier. 320 pp. Love stories by Naiad Press authors.
                                       ISBN 1-56280-074-4   14.95

DAUGHTERS OF A CORAL DAWN by Katherine V. Forrest.
240 pp. Tenth Anniversay Edition.   ISBN 1-56280-104-X   10.95

BODY GUARD by Claire McNab. 208 pp. 6th Carol Ashton
Mystery.   ISBN 1-56280-073-6   10.95

CACTUS LOVE by Lee Lynch. 192 pp. Stories by the beloved
storyteller.   ISBN 1-56280-071-X   9.95

SECOND GUESS by Rose Beecham. 216 pp. 2nd Amanda Valentine
Mystery.   ISBN 1-56280-069-8   9.95

A RAGE OF MAIDENS by Lauren Wright Douglas. 240 pp. 6th Caitlin
Reece Mystery.   ISBN 1-56280-068-X   10.95

TRIPLE EXPOSURE by Jackie Calhoun. 224 pp. Romantic drama
involving many characters.   ISBN 1-56280-067-1   10.95

UP, UP AND AWAY by Catherine Ennis. 192 pp. Delightful
romance.   ISBN 1-56280-065-5   9.95

PERSONAL ADS by Robbi Sommers. 176 pp. Sizzling short
stories.   ISBN 1-56280-059-0   10.95

CROSSWORDS by Penny Sumner. 256 pp. 2nd Victoria Cross
Mystery.   ISBN 1-56280-064-7   9.95

SWEET CHERRY WINE by Carol Schmidt. 224 pp. A novel of
suspense.   ISBN 1-56280-063-9   9.95

CERTAIN SMILES by Dorothy Tell. 160 pp. Erotic short stories.
                                       ISBN 1-56280-066-3   9.95

EDITED OUT by Lisa Haddock. 224 pp. 1st Carmen Ramirez
Mystery.   ISBN 1-56280-077-9   9.95

WEDNESDAY NIGHTS by Camarin Grae. 288 pp. Sexy
adventure.   ISBN 1-56280-060-4   10.95

SMOKEY O by Celia Cohen. 176 pp. Relationships on the
playing field.   ISBN 1-56280-057-4   9.95

KATHLEEN O'DONALD by Penny Hayes. 256 pp. Rose and
Kathleen find each other and employment in 1909 NYC.
                                       ISBN 1-56280-070-1   9.95

STAYING HOME by Elisabeth Nonas. 256 pp. Molly and Alix
want a baby . . . or do they?   ISBN 1-56280-076-0   10.95

TRUE LOVE by Jennifer Fulton. 240 pp. Six lesbians searching
for love in all the "right" places.   ISBN 1-56280-035-3   10.95

KEEPING SECRETS by Penny Mickelbury. 208 pp. 1st Gianna
Maglione Mystery. ISBN 1-56280-052-3 9.95

THE ROMANTIC NAIAD edited by Katherine V. Forrest &
Barbara Grier. 336 pp. Love stories by Naiad Press authors.
ISBN 1-56280-054-X 14.95

UNDER MY SKIN by Jaye Maiman. 336 pp. 3rd Robin Miller
Mystery. ISBN 1-56280-049-3. 10.95

CAR POOL by Karin Kallmaker. 272pp. Lesbians on wheels
and then some! ISBN 1-56280-048-5 10.95

NOT TELLING MOTHER: STORIES FROM A LIFE by Diane
Salvatore. 176 pp. Her 3rd novel. ISBN 1-56280-044-2 9.95

GOBLIN MARKET by Lauren Wright Douglas. 240pp. 5th Caitlin
Reece Mystery. ISBN 1-56280-047-7 10.95

LONG GOODBYES by Nikki Baker. 256 pp. 3rd Virginia Kelly
Mystery. ISBN 1-56280-042-6 9.95

FRIENDS AND LOVERS by Jackie Calhoun. 224 pp. Mid-
western Lesbian lives and loves. ISBN 1-56280-041-8 10.95

THE CAT CAME BACK by Hilary Mullins. 208 pp. Highly
praised Lesbian novel. ISBN 1-56280-040-X 9.95

BEHIND CLOSED DOORS by Robbi Sommers. 192 pp. Hot,
erotic short stories. ISBN 1-56280-039-6 9.95

CLAIRE OF THE MOON by Nicole Conn. 192 pp. See the
movie — read the book! ISBN 1-56280-038-8 10.95

SILENT HEART by Claire McNab. 192 pp. Exotic Lesbian
romance. ISBN 1-56280-036-1 10.95

THE SPY IN QUESTION by Amanda Kyle Williams. 256 pp.
4th Madison McGuire Mystery. ISBN 1-56280-037-X 9.95

SAVING GRACE by Jennifer Fulton. 240 pp. Adventure and
romantic entanglement. ISBN 1-56280-051-5 10.95

CURIOUS WINE by Katherine V. Forrest. 176 pp. Tenth Anniver-
sary Edition. The most popular contemporary Lesbian love story.
ISBN 1-56280-053-1 10.95
　　　　Audio Book (2 cassettes) ISBN 1-56280-105-8 16.95

CHAUTAUQUA by Catherine Ennis. 192 pp. Exciting, romantic
adventure. ISBN 1-56280-032-9 9.95

A PROPER BURIAL by Pat Welch. 192 pp. 3rd Helen Black
Mystery. ISBN 1-56280-033-7 9.95

SILVERLAKE HEAT: A Novel of Suspense by Carol Schmidt.
240 pp. Rhonda is as hot as Laney's dreams. ISBN 1-56280-031-0 9.95

LOVE, ZENA BETH by Diane Salvatore. 224 pp. The most talked
about lesbian novel of the nineties! ISBN 1-56280-030-2 10.95

IN THE GAME by Nikki Baker. 192 pp. 1st Virginia Kelly
Mystery.   ISBN 1-56280-004-3   9.95

STRANDED by Camarin Grae. 320 pp. Entertaining, riveting
adventure.   ISBN 0-941483-99-1   9.95

THE DAUGHTERS OF ARTEMIS by Lauren Wright Douglas.
240 pp. 3rd Caitlin Reece Mystery.   ISBN 0-941483-95-9   9.95

CLEARWATER by Catherine Ennis. 176 pp. Romantic secrets
of a small Louisiana town.   ISBN 0-941483-65-7   8.95

THE HALLELUJAH MURDERS by Dorothy Tell. 176 pp. 2nd
Poppy Dillworth Mystery.   ISBN 0-941483-88-6   8.95

SECOND CHANCE by Jackie Calhoun. 256 pp. Contemporary
Lesbian lives and loves.   ISBN 0-941483-93-2   9.95

BENEDICTION by Diane Salvatore. 272 pp. Striking, contemporary romantic novel.   ISBN 0-941483-90-8   10.95

TOUCHWOOD by Karin Kallmaker. 240 pp. Loving, May/
December romance.   ISBN 0-941483-76-2   9.95

COP OUT by Claire McNab. 208 pp. 4th Carol Ashton Mystery.
                                            ISBN 0-941483-84-3   10.95

THE BEVERLY MALIBU by Katherine V. Forrest. 288 pp. 3rd
Kate Delafield Mystery.   ISBN 0-941483-48-7   11.95

THE PROVIDENCE FILE by Amanda Kyle Williams. 256 pp.
2nd Madison McGuire Mystery.   ISBN 0-941483-92-4   8.95

I LEFT MY HEART by Jaye Maiman. 320 pp. 1st Robin Miller
Mystery.   ISBN 0-941483-72-X   10.95

THE PRICE OF SALT by Patricia Highsmith (writing as Claire
Morgan). 288 pp. Classic lesbian novel, first issued in 1952 . . .
acknowledged by its author under her own, very famous, name.
                                            ISBN 1-56280-003-5   10.95

SIDE BY SIDE by Isabel Miller. 256 pp. From beloved author of
Patience and Sarah.   ISBN 0-941483-77-0   10.95

STAYING POWER: LONG TERM LESBIAN COUPLES by
Susan E. Johnson. 352 pp. Joys of coupledom. ISBN 0-941-483-75-4 14.95

SLICK by Camarin Grae. 304 pp. Exotic, erotic adventure.
                                            ISBN 0-941483-74-6   9.95

NINTH LIFE by Lauren Wright Douglas. 256 pp. 2nd Caitlin
Reece Mystery.   ISBN 0-941483-50-9   9.95

PLAYERS by Robbi Sommers. 192 pp. Sizzling, erotic novel.
                                            ISBN 0-941483-73-8   9.95

MURDER AT RED ROOK RANCH by Dorothy Tell. 224 pp.
1st Poppy Dillworth Mystery.   ISBN 0-941483-80-0   8.95

A ROOM FULL OF WOMEN by Elisabeth Nonas. 256 pp.
Contemporary Lesbian lives.   ISBN 0-941483-69-X   9.95

THEME FOR DIVERSE INSTRUMENTS by Jane Rule. 208 pp.
Powerful romantic lesbian stories.   ISBN 0-941483-63-0   8.95

CLUB 12 by Amanda Kyle Williams. 288 pp. Espionage thriller
featuring a lesbian agent!   ISBN 0-941483-64-9   9.95

DEATH DOWN UNDER by Claire McNab. 240 pp. 3rd Carol
Ashton Mystery.   ISBN 0-941483-39-8   10.95

MONTANA FEATHERS by Penny Hayes. 256 pp. Vivian and
Elizabeth find love in frontier Montana.   ISBN 0-941483-61-4   9.95

LIFESTYLES by Jackie Calhoun. 224 pp. Contemporary Lesbian
lives and loves.   ISBN 0-941483-57-6   10.95

WILDERNESS TREK by Dorothy Tell. 192 pp. Six women on
vacation learning ''new'' skills.   ISBN 0-941483-60-6   8.95

MURDER BY THE BOOK by Pat Welch. 256 pp. 1st Helen
Black Mystery.   ISBN 0-941483-59-2   9.95

THERE'S SOMETHING I'VE BEEN MEANING TO TELL YOU
Ed. by Loralee MacPike. 288 pp. Gay men and lesbians coming out
to their children.   ISBN 0-941483-44-4   9.95

LIFTING BELLY by Gertrude Stein. Ed. by Rebecca Mark. 104 pp.
Erotic poetry.   ISBN 0-941483-51-7   10.95

AFTER THE FIRE by Jane Rule. 256 pp. Warm, human novel by
this incomparable author.   ISBN 0-941483-45-2   8.95

PLEASURES by Robbi Sommers. 204 pp. Unprecedented
eroticism.   ISBN 0-941483-49-5   9.95

EDGEWISE by Camarin Grae. 372 pp. Spellbinding
adventure.   ISBN 0-941483-19-3   9.95

FATAL REUNION by Claire McNab. 224 pp. 2nd Carol Ashton
Mystery.   ISBN 0-941483-40-1   10.95

IN EVERY PORT by Karin Kallmaker. 228 pp. Jessica's sexy,
adventuresome travels.   ISBN 0-941483-37-7   10.95

OF LOVE AND GLORY by Evelyn Kennedy. 192 pp. Exciting
WWII romance.   ISBN 0-941483-32-0   10.95

CLICKING STONES by Nancy Tyler Glenn. 288 pp. Love
transcending time.   ISBN 0-941483-31-2   9.95

SOUTH OF THE LINE by Catherine Ennis. 216 pp. Civil War
adventure.   ISBN 0-941483-29-0   8.95

WOMAN PLUS WOMAN by Dolores Klaich. 300 pp. Supurb
Lesbian overview.   ISBN 0-941483-28-2   9.95

THE FINER GRAIN by Denise Ohio. 216 pp. Brilliant young
college lesbian novel.   ISBN 0-941483-11-8   8.95

BEFORE STONEWALL: THE MAKING OF A GAY AND
LESBIAN COMMUNITY by Andrea Weiss & Greta Schiller.
96 pp., 25 illus.   ISBN 0-941483-20-7   7.95

OSTEN'S BAY by Zenobia N. Vole. 204 pp. Sizzling adventure
romance set on Bonaire.   ISBN 0-941483-15-0   8.95

LESSONS IN MURDER by Claire McNab. 216 pp. 1st Carol Ashton
Mystery.   ISBN 0-941483-14-2   10.95

YELLOWTHROAT by Penny Hayes. 240 pp. Margarita, bandit,
kidnaps Julia.   ISBN 0-941483-10-X   8.95

SAPPHISTRY: THE BOOK OF LESBIAN SEXUALITY by
Pat Califia. 3d edition, revised. 208 pp.   ISBN 0-941483-24-X   10.95

CHERISHED LOVE by Evelyn Kennedy. 192 pp. Erotic Lesbian
love story.   ISBN 0-941483-08-8   10.95

THE SECRET IN THE BIRD by Camarin Grae. 312 pp. Striking,
psychological suspense novel.   ISBN 0-941483-05-3   8.95

TO THE LIGHTNING by Catherine Ennis. 208 pp. Romantic
Lesbian 'Robinson Crusoe' adventure.   ISBN 0-941483-06-1   8.95

DREAMS AND SWORDS by Katherine V. Forrest. 192 pp.
Romantic, erotic, imaginative stories.   ISBN 0-941483-03-7   10.95

MEMORY BOARD by Jane Rule. 336 pp. Memorable novel
about an aging Lesbian couple.   ISBN 0-941483-02-9   12.95

THE ALWAYS ANONYMOUS BEAST by Lauren Wright Douglas.
224 pp. 1st Caitlin Reece Mystery.
                                           ISBN 0-941483-04-5   8.95

MURDER AT THE NIGHTWOOD BAR by Katherine V. Forrest.
240 pp. 2nd Kate Delafield Mystery.   ISBN 0-930044-92-4   11.95

WINGED DANCER by Camarin Grae. 228 pp. Erotic Lesbian
adventure story.   ISBN 0-930044-88-6   8.95

PAZ by Camarin Grae. 336 pp. Romantic Lesbian adventurer
with the power to change the world.   ISBN 0-930044-89-4   8.95

SOUL SNATCHER by Camarin Grae. 224 pp. A puzzle, an
adventure, a mystery — Lesbian romance.   ISBN 0-930044-90-8   8.95

THE LOVE OF GOOD WOMEN by Isabel Miller. 224 pp.
Long-awaited new novel by the author of the beloved *Patience
and Sarah*.   ISBN 0-930044-81-9   8.95

THE LONG TRAIL by Penny Hayes. 248 pp. Vivid adventures
of two women in love in the old west.   ISBN 0-930044-76-2   8.95

These are just a few of the many Naiad Press titles — we are the oldest and
largest lesbian/feminist publishing company in the world. We also offer an
enormous selection of lesbian video products. Please request a complete
catalog. We offer personal service; we encourage and welcome direct mail
orders from individuals who have limited access to bookstores carrying our
publications.